PRAISE FOR

The Melting Season

"At times, *The Melting Season* resembles *Thelma and Louise*. At other times, the novel reads like an updated *Sister Carrie* with Theodore Dreiser's two main characters fused into one. But Attenberg's narrative voice—a lean, straight-ahead, deadpan tone that cuts cleanly through Catherine's hypocrisy and self-pity like a laser-guided strike—makes *The Melting Season* singular and disquieting."   —*Chicago Tribune*

"With a trail of whiskey and Diet Cokes in her wake, Catherine heads west to leave behind a damaged marriage. Reading about her life in Vegas and her road to self-discovery in this novel feels like peeking at a friend's diary."   —*Glamour*

"'*I did not mean to take the money. Well, no*t all o*f it.*' With that intriguing first sentence, Jami Attenberg pulls you into . . . *The Melting Season.* She has a talent for creating strong, interesting characters and situations that keep the story humming along. With this finely tuned story about the power of friendship and the thrill of self-discovery, Attenberg proves she is one of the bright lights of her generation of writers."

—*Chicago Sun-Times*

"Attenberg is a brave, honest writer with scary talent, and this novel about a young woman heading west to escape a failing marriage and a small town is her best yet."

—*Louisville Courier-Journal*

"[Attenberg] renders poignant prose and portrays the desperate behavior of her characters with verve."   —*Booklist*

"Attenberg moves *The Melting Season* along with crisp, gritty, bold words. She doesn't pretty up her main character's demons, which enables the reader to truly get to know this disquieting heroine and pull for her. It's honest, direct, and shows that even difficult, troublesome experiences from the past can still somehow be redeemed in the future. *The Melting Season* is a satisfying, refreshing read—one of the best novels I've read in a very long time. Grade: A."   —*Cincinnati CityBeat*

"An intelligent, moving portrait of a journey to self-awareness, with meaty characters and a refreshing absence of psychobabble."
                                                    —*Kirkus Reviews*

"Jami Attenberg is well on her way to becoming the Joyce Carol Oates of Brooklyn."   —*The Huffington Post*

PRAISE FOR
The Kept Man

"Unabashedly emotional, refreshingly devoid of New York City cynicism, and tenderly funny."   —*People*

"Attenberg has an admirable sense of fun."
                                            —*San Francisco Chronicle*

"Attenberg has a wonderful eye for detail: Her vivid descriptions of Williamsburg—almost a character in itself—are truly engaging."   —*TimeOut New York*

"Like Mary Gaitskill, Attenberg gets at the dark and complex hungers that underlie even the most basic human interactions."
        —Kate Christensen, award-winning author of *The Great Man*

"Jami Attenberg has created a fascinatingly complicated heroine—all at once needy and prickly, frightened and brave. *The Kept Man* becomes a beautifully etched exploration of why we hold on, and how we bring ourselves to let go."
—Leah Stewart, author of *The Myth of You and Me*

"*The Kept Man* is a challenge to apathy—it's a novel about remaining constructive in the face of personal change . . . told with wit and verve."   —*Interview*

"Vibrant, brutal, and beautiful . . . an unforgettable story. *The Kept Man* is a gem."
—Amanda Eyre Ward, author of *How to Be Lost* and *Forgive Me*

"A staggering first novel. It sends you to your thesaurus, hoping to find the best praise: mesmerizing; extraordinary; phenomenal. None of these does this book justice. It's a real triumph by a great talent."
—Darin Strauss, author of *Chang and Eng* and *The Real McCoy*

"A dynamic novel . . . rich in sensual details. Attenberg draws a complicated, pensive, emotional landscape best lived vicariously, through her lens of dreamy language."
—*The Sunday Oregonian*

"*The Kept Man* testifies to the power of human connections."
—*The L Magazine*

ALSO BY JAMI ATTENBERG

Instant Love
The Kept Man

The Melting Season

JAMI ATTENBERG

RIVERHEAD BOOKS

New York

RIVERHEAD BOOKS
Published by the Penguin Group
Penguin Group (USA) Inc.
375 Hudson Street, New York, New York 10014, USA
Penguin Group (Canada), 90 Eglinton Avenue East, Suite 700, Toronto, Ontario M4P 2Y3, Canada
(a division of Pearson Penguin Canada Inc.)
Penguin Books Ltd., 80 Strand, London WC2R 0RL, England
Penguin Group Ireland, 25 St. Stephen's Green, Dublin 2, Ireland (a division of Penguin Books Ltd.)
Penguin Group (Australia), 250 Camberwell Road, Camberwell, Victoria 3124, Australia
(a division of Pearson Australia Group Pty. Ltd.)
Penguin Books India Pvt. Ltd., 11 Community Centre, Panchsheel Park, New Delhi—110 017, India
Penguin Group (NZ), 67 Apollo Drive, Rosedale, North Shore 0632, New Zealand
(a division of Pearson New Zealand Ltd.)
Penguin Books (South Africa) (Pty.) Ltd., 24 Sturdee Avenue, Rosebank, Johannesburg 2196,
South Africa

Penguin Books Ltd., Registered Offices: 80 Strand, London WC2R 0RL, England

This is a work of fiction. Names, characters, places, and incidents either are the product of the author's imagination or are used fictitiously, and any resemblance to actual persons, living or dead, business establishments, events, or locales is entirely coincidental. The publisher does not have any control over and does not assume any responsibility for author or third-party websites or their content.

First Riverhead hardcover edition: January 2010
First Riverhead trade paperback edition: January 2011
Riverhead trade paperback ISBN: 978-1-59448-499-5

The Library of Congress has catalogued the Riverhead hardcover edition as follows:

Attenberg, Jami.
The melting season / Jami Attenberg.
    p.   cm.
ISBN 978-1-59448-896-2
   1. Young women—Fiction.   2. Separated women—Fiction.   3. Friendship—Fiction.
4. Sisters—Fiction.   5. Self-actualization (Psychology)—Fiction.   I. Title.
PS3601.T784M45   2010   2009033715
813'.6—dc22

PRINTED IN THE UNITED STATES OF AMERICA

10   9   8   7   6   5   4   3   2   1

for my friends

Part One

1.

I did not mean to take the money. Well, not *all* of it.

At first it was only a tiny amount, a little cream off the top. I was just trying to store away for the winter. Winters were long in Nebraska. We lived on chicken broth and whiskey and tired-looking vegetables from the grocery store. The wind leveled the cornfields, and the snow skimmed the land like a current across a giant lake. Roads were blocked for weeks. Icicles like enormous daggers gathered on rooftops. We wrapped ourselves in scarves and hats so thick all you could see when you passed your neighbor on the street was another set of eyes peeping back at you. If we left the house at all. Some people slept all day long.

There was a comfort to it, but it made me nervous, too. I needed something to warm myself with. A little bit of money would help.

Every week I took a little bit more and I stacked up the bills in the oven of the apartment I was renting. It was not enough that my husband would be missing it, just enough to keep me happy. Or at least not so miserable.

But then my husband kept on betraying me, and suddenly the little stacks of money were not enough anymore. This feeling rolled all over me on the outside and then it dug itself deep inside me. It was a desperate thing, and I hacked on it, coughing like it was a bitter virus attacking my air. It went on like that for months, my lungs full of a crazy kind of dusty illness. I was on the edge of something dire. All it took was a little push. That was when I realized what needed to happen.

I can take it all and no one can stop me.

And there was nothing left to do afterward but get the hell out of town.

I HAD BEEN DRIVING all day on 80, making my way straight through to Cheyenne, when my phone rang for the first time since I had left town. All around me the air was littered with snowflakes, chunky ones that stuck to the earth and piled up high in every direction. The driving was rough. I took the roads careful and slow. I was the only one out there for hours, further proof that I was out of my mind. I thought about nothing but staying straight and not driving off the road. My truck had snow tires, but still I was terrified. I skidded every few minutes. Whenever that happened

I cursed my husband. I would growl his name: *Thomas Madison*. And then I would skid some more. I could crash at any moment. Sometimes I would fiddle with the radio. There was static, and then country music, and then static again. Jesus talk, here and there. I did this for eight hours. Eight hours of feeling like something bad was going to happen. Something worse than all of the bad stuff that had already happened. And then the phone rang. I guess they finally noticed I was gone.

It was my mother calling. First on the scene, no surprise there. She had always had a special sense for trouble, like some hound dog sniffing for game, only she hunted down misery. I let it ring. I did not have a thing to say to anybody, except maybe to Jenny. Poor Jenny, who I had left behind in her own mess. If there was anything I wished I could change it was leaving that girl. The phone went to voice mail. That goddamn deluxe cell phone with video and Internet and all that crap I did not need but my husband had bought for me anyway. Because he had to buy everything fancy and new. It rang again. It went on like that for twenty miles or so, me driving slow, snow beating down, phone ringing on repeat, until finally I picked it up.

"I told you to watch it," she said. "I told you not to go there, but you didn't listen. Twenty-five years old and you've already ruined the rest of your life. Nice work."

I bet there was a can of beer in front of her, halfway down to empty. And a new pack of cigarettes, the plastic wrap crumpled next to it. Still, her lipstick would match her housedress. She was just getting her afternoon buzz on, is all. By the time my father got home from work she would look just like anyone else.

"I did not do anything wrong," I said.

My mother laughed, and it was mean.

"Here's a question for you. Do you think what you did was right?"

I hung up the phone, and then I turned off the power because I knew she would just keep calling. She had all the time in the world.

BY THE TIME I hit Cheyenne all I wanted to do was drink whiskey and eat a cheeseburger. I missed the cheeseburgers from the diner downstairs below my apartment, the ones Papi made for me. I ate there practically every day for months, after my husband kicked me out of the house. Papi made them rare and red for me. I wondered if I would ever have one again.

I found a motel a few exits after the one for downtown Cheyenne. It was cheap and family-owned. Family-owned would have been a comfort in my own town, but on the road it was questionable. I did not know this family, after all. What were they like? I could not drive any farther though. There were some trailers parked out front. Everyone was hiding from the storm. There was a bar next to the hotel that served food, and the girl who checked me in reminded me of Jenny, how she could be so excited and sullen at the same time, like she was just ready to burst. I felt like I would be safe for the night. I filled out some paperwork. I used my married name, then stopped myself, but it was too late. It would look weird if I crossed out my own name and started over so I kept it. Then the girl asked me for my credit card.

"I want to pay in cash," I said. I knew enough not to leave a credit card trail behind me. Every cop show I had ever watched since I was a kid had taught me that.

"You won't get charged," she said. "It's just for incidentals."

Incidental, I liked that word. Something could happen at any moment. An *incident*.

"What kind of incidentals?" I said.

"Well, we've got microwave popcorn if you get the snackers after the bar is closed, and there's dirty movies on channel eighteen if you're into that." She sneered a little bit.

"Good to know," I said coolly. I would not be cowed by a child.

In the room I shoved the suitcase of cash under the bed. The suitcase was made of red leather. I had only used it once before, on my honeymoon. After that, there was no reason to. We had never left town again. I spent my whole life in the same place, with the same people. I never thought I needed to go anywhere. And yet there I was, getting away as fast as I could.

I collapsed on the bed and turned on the TV. To just not have to think for a while, that was what I wanted.

I flipped to an entertainment news show. There was always one on for me, no matter what time of day. There were two hosts, one with dark spiky hair, and one with blond spiky hair. The one with blond spiky hair was break-dancing. The one with dark spiky hair said, "You sure love to pop and lock, don't you?" The one with blond spiky hair yelled, "You know it." The dark-haired man grinned, turned to another camera, and said, "And now it's time for rehab watch!"

The two hosts talked for a while about who was in and out of rehab. There was a tiny image of a revolving door whipping around on the bottom right corner of the screen. They were being funny, but they were assholes, too.

"And finally, we've got an off-the-wagon alert," said the dark-haired host. A swirling police light went off in the back of the studio and an alarm started to ring.

The blond guy covered his ears and grinned.

And there was footage of my all-time favorite TV-movie-of-the-week star, Rio DeCarlo, stumbling out of a limousine and into a security guard's arms. A whirlwind of flashbulbs went off and she covered her eyes with her hands and rushed through the crowd and into a hotel.

"Her rep says seasickness," said the dark-haired host.

"Seasickness?"

"And Dramamine."

"Dramamine." The blond host smiled slyly.

"She was on a yacht all day."

"You know, she's just two visits shy of our Rehab Hall of Fame."

"That's going to be an exciting day."

I threw the remote control at the TV set. I hoped it *was* Dramamine. I hoped she was going to make it. I wanted someone in this world to make it. I was not sure right then if it could be me.

Then I took a shower for the first time in a week. All I had been doing was sitting around being mad at the world. There had been a lot going on, but it had all been in my head. A shower had not occurred to me the entire time.

The hot water ran out quickly. The radiator near the window banged and moaned. The windows steamed up. It reminded me of nothing in particular but still it felt familiar. I wiped the steam off the mirror with the towel and stared at myself. My hair in damp tangles all over my shoulders, the pink puffed-out rims of my eyes, a jag of tiny red pimples across my nose.

I needed sleep.

The comforter on the bed was brown and there were tiny cartoon trains all over it. It itched my skin when I slid underneath it. I put my head down and slept for an hour. When I woke my hair was dry and clean. I felt rested. I still had the same feeling as when I was driving, that something was going to happen, but now it could go either way. I thought about playing hide-and-seek with my sister, Jenny, when we were still kids, her barely reading her storybooks by herself, me on the verge of being a teenager. I would always hide from her. This was how I babysat. Nothing too fancy. I hid, she ran around the house yelling my name. Boy, could she hustle. But she loved it, it was her favorite game to play, and I guess I did not mind it that much either. I remember sitting in the closet, her about to open the door. I never knew what I was going to do. I could pounce or I could scream or I could jump in the air and laugh. But something had to happen next.

I put on a few layers of clothes. I missed my summertime tan, and my short skirts, and how happy and free the air on my skin made me feel. I brushed my hair. It was blond and thick and spread out over my shoulders and down my back to my waist. My crown of glory, just as it had been for years. I looked at myself in the mirror. I was thinner, like a scrawny child now, tiny bones, my flesh lost to stress and misery. But I had the same face, and my beloved hair. I still looked like me. Only I was not Moonie Madison anymore.

I had been Moonie since high school. When Thomas first fell in love with me, he named me that. I was his moon, and he was my stars, that is the way it was right from the beginning. Just like that I was Moonie. No one else. During our wedding Thomas even said, "I take you, Moonie—I mean Catherine," and everyone laughed. But it was all true. I did not even remember who I was before I met him.

And now I was not Moonie anymore. Catherine did not feel too right either. I had already stopped being Catherine. I was going to have to sort out a whole new me.

I left the room and locked the door behind me. The door next to mine cracked open, and I saw a woman watching me. I thought maybe she was like me for a second, traveling alone. But then the door swung open and a little boy came running out. He was a toddler, wearing just diapers on his bottom half and a sweater on top. The woman plucked him up and clutched him to her chest. I could not decide how old she was. Everything about her looked the same as me, except for her forehead. There were lines carved into it like rivers in the earth. I wondered what it would feel like, to rub my hands along those lines. This is how we are different, I thought. I am still smooth, and you are lined. I wondered if she hated having them, or even if she noticed them at all. I wondered if that little boy was why she had those lines, if the love she felt for him was so strong and deep that her face had changed forever. She smiled at me, and then the baby started crying, and she closed the door.

I went to the bar. I could not remember ever going to a bar by myself. That seemed like a thing a girl who was looking for trouble would do, and I had never once looked for trouble in my life. The bar was full of men, a few guys younger than me, but most of them were in their forties or older. In the back I saw a couple of women with their husbands, and there was a little girl running around who had sparkly barrettes crooked in her hair. I was sure that everyone knew everyone else. Most people were smoking. In certain parts of the bar the air was so thick with it you could not see people's faces clearly. I did not want to eat there, but I was starving.

I sat at the bar. The stool had a tear in it. The men to the right of me were laughing and seemed harmless enough. They were not any different from the men who came into the diner back home, men who had known me since I was a kid. My father did not take me into bars when I was growing up, but he was not the kind to go out and socialize. Working all day at the pharmacy was enough people time for him. He was not a snob, though, and he did not raise one either. I sat down and ordered a Southern Comfort and Diet Coke from the bartender, a short woman with breasts so big it was like there was no stomach left. They just took over everything. Her lipstick stained the skin around her mouth where age was fading her. She had the same eyes as the girl who had checked me in at the motel. She could be complaining one minute, she could make you laugh the next. You just didn't know what you would get from her.

I turned around on my stool and faced the room. Most people nodded at me; a few smiled. I smiled back. I watched as a young guy with sloppy lips made his way around the room. Every few minutes, he would lean in too close to someone and yell, "Head butt." Then he would do just that, slam his head against someone else's. There would be this loud crack, and people would turn and stare, then go back to their talking. This was his thing, I guessed.

"Don't worry, sweetheart, he won't do it to you," said the man next to me. He had long feathery hair that was brittle on the edges. He wore a leather vest and his skin was pitted and rotting, but he had a nice light in his eyes. I liked looking at him. "He only does it to people he knows.

Especially he's not going to do it to a girl like you." He blew smoke from his cigarette away from my face. "You just passing through or you're staying awhile or . . ."

"I just came to get some food," I said. "It's been a long day of driving."

"Oh yeah? Where you headed?"

"West," I said. And then I added, "Los Angeles," because it was as far west as I could think to go. It sounded like a place you moved to when you needed to start over. It was a lie, but there was no way I could tell the truth. And maybe it could become the truth. There were a lot of options. The world was wide open in front of me. I would have to trust myself to find the way.

The man introduced himself. His name was Arnold. He and I talked about the roads for a little while. He and his son, Pete, had just come back from Denver, visiting Arnold's ex-wife and Pete's mother. They rode their motorcycles, and things had been rough with the snow. He told me to just keep heading west, to take 80 through Salt Lake City and head down to Vegas. If I kept the pedal to the metal, I could make it there in a day. Pete came over and introduced himself to me. He was tall and his face had not been ruined by drink yet. His hair was tied back in a ponytail and he had long sideburns. He was rough-looking, for sure, but I did not mind talking to him. I had spent so many years with Thomas, who could be so weepy and sensitive, that it was nice to talk to men who did not look like they had ever cried.

Arnold and Pete took turns buying me SoCo and Diet

Cokes. The drinks tasted like syrup, and I took big gulps of them like medicine. They treated me like I was really interesting, but in fact they were doing most of the talking. There was nothing I could tell them about anyway without getting myself in trouble.

Arnold started in on this story about how his ex-wife had left him and Pete years ago, when Pete was still a baby, but how they were all still close. Arnold was part Arapaho, and when he and his wife, Trinie, were married they moved onto a reservation nearby. Trinie had been a dance student in Colorado and had dreamed of moving to New York, but had gotten pregnant with Pete almost immediately after she met Arnold. Neither one of them could afford much. Trinie's parents had kicked her out of the house when they found out she was pregnant with some half-breed's kid, and all Arnold's folks could do was find them a small farmhouse deep in the woods of the reservation that they could rent for cheap. It was three miles to the main road, and Arnold rode his Harley into work as a day laborer and left Trinie there alone to take care of little Pete. Once every few weeks Arnold's mother would drive Trinie into town to buy groceries in her pickup truck, but mostly Trinie was alone all day long, just her and the baby.

At first she liked it: she had a vegetable garden, and she learned to chop wood. "She was becoming one with the earth," said Arnold. She used to put on little dance performances in the trees for Arnold and baby Pete. But eventually the isolation began to drive her nuts.

I thought about me and Thomas out on our farm, with

no one to talk to but each other, even with all those construction workers hammering in the background. They were building us our brand-new dream farmhouse, even though I was just fine with the way it was. He said it was necessary. He said we deserved it. He said he wanted to treat me right. So I let Thomas run the show, and I stayed away from all the renovation business. And once he started fixing things up, he could not stop. Soon enough he was making changes to himself, but by then it was too late for me to stop him. I let him be in charge, until I could not stand it anymore.

"I bet she went crazy out there," I said.

"Crazy's a word I'd use," he said.

She begged Arnold to move but he would not listen. He liked the quiet, dark woods, and coming home to his wife and child in his cozy cabin. It felt safe and nice to him. He was not hearing a thing she said. Trinie let her dark hair grow long and it fell below her waist. She started to stage small acts of defiance. She cooked meat only halfway through for dinner sometimes, at least the meat she served to her husband, and she taught her child new and unusual curses to say to his father, as if he were the parrot of a salty old fisherman.

Arnold shook his head and laughed when he told me that last part, and there was a forgiving glint in his eye. It probably took her forever to get him going, I thought. He would have let her keep torturing him till the end. Pete got up to get me another drink. I was getting good and drunk. I realized I had forgotten to eat but I was not hungry anymore. Arnold said something to me about how his house was nicer than any old hotel, and if I wanted I could come out and stay with the two of them. Off in the corner there was another crack of one head against another, and then somebody started yelling. Pete came back and handed me a drink, then put his hand around my neck and rubbed the muscles there until they were warm. It had been a while since someone had touched me like that and I was enjoying it a little bit. Arnold watched Pete rubbing me for a minute. His face did not change at all. Then he motioned for me to move in closer to him, and I did, and Pete's hand dropped away.

"The last straw—for Trinie, not for me, I would have let her stay forever no matter what she did to me, I mean she's my wife and the mother of my son, come on—was the blizzard of . . . was it '83? Could it have been that long?" Arnold paused and scratched his chin, and did some thinking. In the corner a man lost another game of pool and threw his cue on the table. I realized everyone around me was drunk, too. It was getting late. The families had packed up their kids and left by then, and the only other woman left was the bartender.

"I think it was '83," said Pete. He slipped his hand around my waist. "You sure you want to stay in that hotel tonight?" he said in my ear. I did not answer him.

The blizzard came and it was a whiteout for days. There was no work to be found so Arnold and Trinie were trapped in the house with little Pete. It was cold and they were running out of wood so they used it sparingly. No one wanted to go outside in that weather and chop. And that one extra person around all the time made the house feel even smaller to Trinie. Plus Arnold was bored. He went through a few fifths of whiskey a day. They started yelling and fighting and no one could hear her scream. "She kept screaming," said Arnold. "Hoping someone would come and save her or pull her out of there, and the more she screamed the more she realized she was in the middle of nowhere. Then she got it in her head that if no one could hear her scream, no one would hear *me* scream. She decided to test that little theory of hers out."

Next to me Pete nodded twice, and left his head down.

Trinie went after Arnold with an ax one morning. He woke up just as she lowered it and he rolled off to the side and onto the floor. The ax went through the bed. Pete saw the whole thing.

"I don't remember much but I remember that," said Pete.

"After that we sent her back to Colorado to stay with her parents. They were ready to have her back, as long as I stayed away." Arnold started laughing. "And believe me, at the time I thought: you can keep her."

A fight started in the corner by the pool table. Men tumbled over each other like children and then they were both shoved outside and the whole bar emptied to watch them. We all carried our drinks with us. I slipped a little bit on a patch of ice and Pete caught me. The snow was falling lighter and the sky was finally dark. There were grunts and punches and people casually stared. No one wanted it to get too crazy, but no one wanted it to stop either. It was a snowstorm, there wasn't much else to do but drink and fight. There was blood on the snow and one man finally passed out. We all shuffled back in the bar.

"I saw that she was right, of course, but by then it was too late," said Arnold.

"We got a new house down the road from here," said Pete. "Right in the middle of it all."

"I have to go home," I said.

"We'll walk you back to your room," said Arnold.

"It is okay," I said. "I am fine."

"We can't have you slipping and falling in the snow," said Arnold. "Come on, Pete, give her a hand." Pete put his hand under my elbow. We made our way back toward my room. My eyes were closing down on my face. Arnold was saying something to me; I could hear him through my eyes.

"You sure you have to leave tomorrow?" he said. "It'd be nice to see your face around longer."

"You sure are pretty," said Pete.

I did not want to hurt their feelings. They had been so nice to me. And they had spent all that money on my drinks. I felt bad for them, too, that Trinie had left them alone in the woods. Arnold put his hand around my other elbow. They were both treating me like I could not walk at all, but I knew that I could.

"I can walk," I said. I tried to shrug them off but they would not let me go. "I am fine," I said. We were almost to my door and I just wanted to get under the covers and go to sleep by myself.

"We're just trying to help you out," said Arnold.

"I think you might be a little drunk there, sweetheart," said Pete.

"I am not," I mumbled, though I knew I was.

Pete and Arnold rested me against the door. They both moved in closer toward me.

"I just don't know," said Pete. "You look like you need a hand to me. Don't you think, Dad?"

"Where's your key?" said Arnold. "We'll get you into bed."

"I am fine," I said.

"Just give us the key," said Arnold.

"I am fine," I said louder.

"There ain't no need to yell," said Arnold. "There's people sleeping."

"I am fine," I yelled.

Pete lifted his hand, and it seemed like he was going to clamp it across my mouth. But he just scratched his head with it instead. Next door a light went on. We all turned. A hand pulled the curtain to the side, and two sets of eyes peered at us. Pete and Arnold took a step back.

"Everything's fine," said Arnold.

I pulled out my key and it dropped to the ground and Pete leaned forward to help but Arnold put a hand on him and pulled him back. I picked it up off the snow. My hand burned with the chill of it. I let myself into my room, and when I looked back, Arnold and Pete were just standing there. Arnold's hand was still on Pete, holding him back.

"You sure you're okay?" said Pete. It was a desperate whine, like a stray dog looking for food or the touch of a hand.

"I am fine," I said, and I closed the door. I locked it. I did not take my clothes off or anything. Tomorrow I will be a new me, I thought. I need to figure out how to be a new me. I got under the covers, and when my heart stopped racing through my chest, then, at last, I could sleep.

2.

My cell phone woke me up early, not even 6 A.M. I was miserable, my head swollen with alcohol, the spot behind my eyes tender and on fire. I checked the phone. It was a video from my sister, Jenny. She was standing sideways in front of a mirror, her stomach puffed out, completely pregnant. My heart stopped right there in Cheyenne, Wyoming. Then she pulled out a pillow, showing me the little bump left behind, and started laughing.

Hilarious, I texted her. She should take that act on the road. She would make millions.

She texted back: *When are you coming home?*

I did not reply because I did not have an answer. If I was coming home at all. My phone buzzed again. Jenny had sent me a picture of our garbage can, a mountain of empty beer cans sprouting out of the top of it. Oh Lord, I thought. Our mother's been drinking more than ever. Still it was not enough for me to turn around home. I could not say one way or the other what I was going to do next, except keep on driving.

Outside the roads were still silent, and the sun rimmed the curtains of the motel room shyly. For a minute I could have been back on the farm, waiting for the rooster to let us know it was time to get up and shake off the night. Some mornings, I would rise before the rooster. But I would let him go first into the day. I did not want to hurt his feelings. There was no one around in the mornings, except me and my husband and the rooster and all his chicken wives. All of us kept close together on that farm. We were not going anywhere.

Then I remembered: my husband had cast me out. No crow to cradle me now. There was a roof over my head, but still I was homeless. The last nine months I had lived in that house it had been a construction zone. Thomas could not wait to spend his daddy's money on renovations once he died. It was the first thing he did after we moved in, call up his high school buddies and put them to work. Work, if you want to call it that. They were sucking Thomas dry just like they sucked those cans of Budweiser all day long, making noises every hour or so like they were lifting something heavy. Tall, strong men strutting and braying like that cock in the morning, Thomas letting them because they were big men now. They had always been bigger than Thomas. It was not hard.

But it was the place I called home. My marital home.

And every bed I had slept in since I would wake up in the night and feel like I was sliding off. I held on to the bed in the motel room in Cheyenne. I grabbed the sheets and pinched the end of the mattress. I was homeless and love-less and all alone in the world.

I allowed myself one more minute of feeling sorry for myself, and then I snapped up out of bed. I had to get roll-ing. There was nothing for me in Cheyenne except a place to hide.

I showered off the smoke from last night; I could smell it rising in the steam around me. Then I threw away the clothes I had worn. I could not imagine packing them next to my other clothes. The smoke would infect everything. I almost threw up, thinking about the smoke and Pete and Arnold, the crack of heads together, the fall of the ax, the blood on the snow. I felt a clenching deep inside me. If that woman had not looked through the window just then, those two could have been thrashing around on top of me soon enough. Heavy and mean. Father and son taking turns. It was just plain wrong how pushy they had been at the end there. It was all rushing through my brain.

I closed the door behind me and walked toward the lobby to drop off the key, my shoes crunching on the fresh snow left behind from last night's storm. I was the only one up at the motel. I could see bloodstains mixed in with the snow in front of the bar. I pushed the key through a slot in the front door of the lobby. There was a tiny squeak and then it snapped shut.

I need to be quieter and calmer, I thought. For years

I was silent and hidden away on that farm, tending to Thomas's needs, and now I could not shut myself up. There I was, getting into trouble with strangers, yelling in the middle of the night. What was I doing? I needed to be careful. There might be people looking for me. I began to feel uncomfortable and thick with guilt, even though I did not believe I had done anything wrong. I was worried I was still drunk, but I got in the truck anyway. I cursed myself, and then I started the engine.

Route 80 was still pretty messed up from the weather. Great hills of snow were pushed to the sides like silent guards standing watch. I prayed for safe passage. The land started to change as I drove farther west. It was raining and the snow had melted some and I could see that the land was curvier, more luscious. Everything in my hometown was flat and remained the same, except for the corn, growing, growing, and then gone again. I had never considered the earth could be any other way. Why would I need to think about that? I was never leaving.

The farthest I had ever been away was during my honeymoon, six years past already. We went to a resort town on a lake in Minnesota because that is where my parents went on their honeymoon, and they were paying the bills. They sat us down at the kitchen table the night of our engagement barbecue in the backyard. My dad handed the envelope with the tickets to my mother, who slid them across the kitchen table to us. "We had some magical nights there," she said drily. "It's good for swimming," said my dad. He put his hand on my mother's shoulder, and she turned her eyes at it and stared dully, until he pulled it back again.

If it had been left up to me and Thomas we probably would have stayed home and snuggled up in bed for a week straight, watching TV, renting movies, me making popcorn and grilled cheese sandwiches. Easy stuff we could eat in bed. I was not even sure we needed a wedding. That seemed like extra to me. But you do not look a gift horse in the mouth, Thomas whispered in my ear later, after they handed us the envelope. And it would be our only chance to see a little of the world. Because Thomas had only ever promised to show me his love.

The resort itself was like a pioneer village. Everyone had their own little log cabin, all of them circling a lake like we were settlers keeping each other company in the wilderness. We had the honeymoon suite so there were fuzzy slippers and bathrobes waiting for us and chocolate roses and a bottle of champagne in the kitchen.

"Ooh la la," said Thomas, and he popped a rose in his mouth. He did a little dance over to me and said, "Come here and I'll give you a chocolate kiss." We put our arms around each other and I let him put his tongue deep into my mouth. It tasted like chocolate but also the peanuts we had been snacking on all day during the drive. I liked the saltiness but it was not what I was expecting. I guess he could tell. He pulled back from me. I could see how wounded he was. I decided not to say no to him for the rest of the seven days and six nights we were there.

Later that night he pushed into me over and over again

and I gasped out of love and he said, "Don't lie," and I said, "I'm not, it's good to be next to you, it makes me feel good to have our bodies naked together," and he pushed in harder, banged up against me. I knew I would be bruised in the morning. He did it like that sometimes when he was drunk. But I let it go, I let him go at it, because I wanted him to be happy.

The next morning, Thomas and I walked down the waterfront to see how we were going to kill the next seven days. I saw a waterslide in the distance, and Thomas pointed out the kayaks on the lake. That was the first time I realized that it was a strange place for us to go on our honeymoon, if we were going somewhere at all. We grew up in a state that was practically dry. What did we care about the water? Sure I liked the community pool in the summertime, but that was all we could do at the resort, roll around in the hay at night, and play in the water during the day. And I think there were supposed to be some hiking trails but I was not much of a walker anymore. I had my truck by then. I just liked rattling along the cornfields. There were no cornfields here. There were thick green trees and the water and the air smelled nice, murky and earthy at the same time, but I did not know what to do with myself for even a second.

Thomas had the answer though. He took my hand and pulled me along to a dock where there were sailboats floating at the end, all tied up next to each other.

"We should rent one of these," he said. He looked out

at the lake, at another sailboat skimming the water like a bird. "We should go sailing."

"Thomas Madison, I've known you practically my whole life and you do not know how to sail," I said, and I laughed.

He looked at me, and he squinted his eyes. I had done it, pissed him off, on the first real day of our honeymoon.

"I do too know how to sail. My dad taught me. He was in the Coast Guard, and he knew how, and he took me sailing a few times. It was when he and Mom were still together. We went on vacation." He looked dreamy for a second. "In Wisconsin."

"All right, I guess I did not know that part," I mumbled.

"Aw, it's okay, honey," he said. He put his arm around me. "Don't feel bad you don't know it all yet. You will." He steered me toward the man renting the sailboats, a rough, red-faced man, with grizzly gray hair covering his chin and racing up his cheeks. Half burned by the sun, half burned by age. He wore a yellow T-shirt that said, "Sunny Day Sailboats" in blue letters.

Thomas and Mr. Sunny Day set to negotiating about the boats. I watched Thomas closely. We never left our town, ever, barely talked to people we did not know. Maybe a few times a year I would meet someone new. Making new friends did not seem important to me then. We had everything we needed. But seeing Thomas out in the world was fascinating to me. How he treated people, at first glance, without knowing anything about someone. I just let him do the talking. I was so young then, I thought that was the way. And it was easier, to let someone take care of you.

So there he was, barking at Mr. Sunny Day, who was asking Thomas what he knew about sailing.

"I trained with my father, a former soldier in the U.S. Coast Guard," he said. He had his arms crossed in front of him and his short legs were spread squat. "Since I was a kid I been on the water."

The man backed down a little bit, pulled his body back, kicked the ground with his foot. "Well, I didn't know that, now did I?" he said. He smiled. "Not everyone knows how to handle a boat."

"Oh yeah," said Thomas. "I'm a master tacker."

"All right, then," said Mr. Sunny Day. He and Thomas walked off together and started looking at boats. There was some paperwork he handed to Thomas to sign. Thomas did not read it, just signed it. I shrugged. I twirled my wedding ring around my finger. I squinted out at the lake. Two teenage boys paddled next to each other in kayaks. They were laughing. They wore life vests, so I knew they were safe. It looked calm enough out there on the water, a nice place to be a married couple. The water was a dark purple blue and there were all kinds of living things buzzing in and around it. I slapped a mosquito off me. I wondered how deep the water was. I wondered if it was possible to drown if our sailboat sank. Not that my husband would sink it. Because he had been sailing since he was a child. I had just heard him say it.

Thomas and the man shook hands and Thomas motioned me over. Mr. Sunny Day handed us both life vests,
and we walked toward the boat we would be renting. The
sailboat was a bright fake yellow, stretching to look like
sunshine. "We are newlyweds," I told Mr. Sunny Day,
even though he had not asked.

"Are you now," he said. He held my arm as I got on the
boat. Thomas was already untying the sail. "Just like I
remember," he said. I ducked my head down and slid in
facing Thomas, who was standing knee deep and then
waist high in the water as he pushed us farther out.

"So we'll see you around noon, then," said Mr. Sunny
Day. "Come in and get yourself a nice lunch up at the
lodge. Do yourself a favor and try their Black Angus burgers. Big as your head."

But Thomas was not hearing a thing. He was already
off dreaming on the water, it was just a matter of catching
the right wind. I sat and looked at him, my belly and
breasts pressed up against the life vest. It was hard to
breathe for a second. Mr. Sunny Day stood on the dock
watching us, his hands on his hips, a weird grin on his face.
His legs were skinny and hairless at the top, I noticed that.
And his shorts were too short for a man his age. Out on the
water the two boys kayaking started splashing each other
with their paddles until one of them yelled, "Quit it!"

Thomas got on the boat and it rocked a bit. I thought
for sure we were going down. I closed my eyes and sucked
in my breath and prayed for my husband to be strong, out
on the water, out in the world. And then I opened my eyes

and we were sailing! We were floating so free, me and him, Moonie and Thomas, stars, sun, moon, water, mountain, trees, bees, birds, him and me.

We floated around for an hour like that, not saying much, just beaming at each other. I allowed myself to lie back and take off my life vest and T-shirt, my new pink-striped bikini underneath. Thomas had not seen it yet and his eyes got big and he let out a dirty little laugh. My hair was up in a ponytail and Thomas told me to take it down so I did, and the wind blew it back around me. I felt famous.

"You are gorgeous," said Thomas.

"Thanks, sailor," I said.

We made our way around the lake and looked at all the other log cabins. We waved to some little kids messing around at the shore, building little castles out of empty beer cans. Near the quieter end I could see a deer standing at the edge of some trees. I got excited. I had seen deer before but never while sitting on a yellow sailboat being steered by my new husband.

I started thinking about how we could make sailing our new hobby. Maybe someday we would be able to afford our own sailboat. Maybe we could come back here every year on our anniversary. It was not the worst thing in the world, leaving home every so often. And the way the air felt on that lake, brushing all over my bare skin. The way Thomas looked at me. It was love. I was not yet twenty years old.

As we sailed back toward the dock, Mr. Sunny Day, and

all his sailboats, I felt calm. I closed my eyes and listened
to the rush of the water, the smooth lap against the bottom
of the boat. Thomas was sailing faster. I could hear the
wind beating against the sail. We were in a race with
something. I sat up and looked at Thomas, his face set like
stone, his short legs flexing and folding as he wrestled
with the sail. He had gotten a crew cut for the wedding, so
he even looked like a sailor. The wind picked up a little
more and Thomas howled at it. He was just a boy becoming a man. That is all he was trying to be, was a man.

I wanted to reach out toward him and touch his face
and hands and chest, but he was busy with the sail. I
looked back toward the shore. We were coming up fast.

"Thomas," I said. "Slow it down."

"I'm trying," he said.

Mr. Sunny Day was on the dock, waving his arms at us.
Then, as he saw how fast we were coming in, he sped up
his arms, as if waving them faster could somehow make
us go slower. Then he started motioning us to the right,
away from the dock. I felt the tickle of a laugh in my
throat. I mean it was funny, wasn't it? That we were about
to fuck up this boat. And then I got afraid real fast.

"Tommy, should I jump?" I do not know why I called
him "Tommy" just then. I guess I felt like I was a little
girl and he was a little boy.

"I don't know," said Thomas. He was frantically grab-
bing at the sail, trying to turn it in any direction other
than the one it was going in, but the sail was not having

it. We raced toward the dock. I was frozen: stay or jump, where should I go? What should I do? I should stay with Thomas. I will stay with my husband.

The boat hit the dock in three places, on the front, then it bounced back and hit the side and the sail, which came tumbling down almost on top of Mr. Sunny Day, but he ran off at the last minute. The sound the body of the boat made was kind of awesome. It was a serious crunch, and it rippled through the whole boat, and then it stopped, everything stopped. The sail was dangling over our heads, the boat was dented in pretty serious in the front, and Thomas and I were just sitting there wondering what to do next. I could hear Mr. Sunny Day cursing from the land. "You son of a bitch," he yelled.

There was some arguing after that and I walked back to the cabin by myself because I did not want to see my new husband be crushed like a stubborn hard-backed beetle under Mr. Sunny Day's foot, over and over until he was broken down. I sat in the living room of our log cabin and looked up all around at the paintings of the lakes on the walls, little price tags in the corners, the humming ceiling fan we had not minded the night before but that now seemed louder than an airplane overhead, the well-worn quilt with blocks of stars, the chocolate roses, the empty bottle of champagne, and our suitcases, still halfway packed. I memorized my honeymoon suite because I knew we would be leaving before the day was done. Out in the world, my husband crashed the first thing he touched. But at home, he would be in control and we would be safe, and I wanted more than anything to be safe in my new hus-band's arms.

We will just stay put, then, I thought at the time. And so we did.

3.

Salt Lake City was seventy miles away, and suddenly it was forty, and then it was ten, and there were signs for Cedar City and Las Vegas, too. There were mountains all around, biggest things I had ever seen, clawing their way up to the sky. Then in the middle of nowhere, in the middle of the earth, was a huge stretch of highways that circled the city, and tall buildings sparkling in the blinding light of the winter sun. For a while, I let my eyes wander through the city, and then there they were again in the distance, even more mountains, choked with blue at the base, and white caps on top spreading down to the middle. I felt a little pull in my throat. I had seen natural beauty in the past but it had been so long since I had stopped to consider it. I saw things the way Thomas did, or we talked about them together and came to the same conclusion. Now I had to figure it all out on my own. The mountains were alive and changing all the time and getting older but still starting things brand-new. The rocks and the dirt and the earth had been there forever, but the snow had probably fallen just that morning. No one judged those mountains for a thing, I thought. However they changed, in however many years or if it were in an instant, people would still find them beautiful.

I decided to push through to Las Vegas. I was being chased. I was chasing something. I could not get out of the car.

As I drove, the land changed again. It was cold and there was snow for a long time, and then it all started to thin out, and then soon enough I was in the desert. There was sand and sage and wide skies and every corner I turned, the earth just seemed to get prettier, until I found myself smiling. It was the first time I had smiled without faking it in what seemed like months. Maybe I was going to be okay, I thought.

And then there I was, in Las Vegas. I drove down the main strip slowly. I did not think it would be possible to ever go fast there. The streets were clogged with taxis mostly, but also buses and vans and cars with license plates from all over the country, though most of all from California. I will admit to being shocked by it all, though I felt dumb for it. How many times had I seen Las Vegas on TV in my life? I should have known by then what to expect.

Still Las Vegas looked like nonsense to me, a cartoon

version of a real town. I knew buildings came from somewhere, that they did not just pop up out of thin air. But it
seemed like Las Vegas was made from scratch. There was
nothing all around for miles, and then all of a sudden
there were these huge towers that were imitations of real
places. There was a circus, and there was ancient Rome,
and there was the Eiffel Tower. Somebody built these, I
kept thinking. Where I came from all the buildings were
small and made sense. They served a purpose. This seemed
almost immoral. But I could not say I minded it either.
Everything new I saw made me feel like I was on the way
to figuring myself out.

It was just before the sunset when I arrived. I moved
with the traffic, slowly jerking forward. On the sidewalks
all around people walked slowly, like it was summertime,
and they were taking their evening stroll. A car behind
me started honking and I covered my outside ear with one
hand. I did not know where to stop. I opened the window
and it was cool, but the sun felt nice on my skin. The air
felt still and clean. This is one reason people came here to
get away from it all, I thought. Sunshine in December,
God Bless America.

My parents had come here once in the winter. It was
one of Dad's pharmaceutical conferences. They did not
travel much. My father was like most everyone else in
town, just like I was. Not much in a hurry to go anywhere.
Simply content. My mother was mixed, and I was always
confused by it. Sometimes she was herky-jerky all over the

place, wishing she was anywhere but our town. She had
had big dreams once. She had been to France once, she
would have you know. That's right. France. In Europe. But
as I got older, and especially after Jenny was born, she
pushed all of that down, deep down. The balance shifted
somewhere along the way, and she just became our mother
and not much more than that. She had her reasons, even
if it was not always clear to us what they were. Whatever
else she had imagined she would do with her life seemed
to be gone forever, or at least hidden so far away none of
us ever saw it.

Still she liked her trips when she got them, and Las
Vegas was a knockout, as far as she was concerned. I was
in high school, and they left me in charge of Jenny. I sat
in the room while my mother packed, and she told me
she was taking her "dancing shoes." I remember listening to her, and being happy for her, but in the back of
my mind I was happier for Thomas. I knew he would be
glad they were going away. He wanted to sleep in my bed
with me, like a real man. He could spend the night at
last. We had tickled each other in the mornings and paid
Jenny twenty bucks to keep her mouth shut. I made blue-
berry pancakes and sausage for everyone. My parents
came back two days later tired but still hungry for each
other's kisses. My father stroked the back of my mother's
neck at dinner. It was one of the few times I can remember bliss in that house. Everyone was happy all at once.
I prayed Las Vegas might have some healing powers for

me, but I could not imagine sleeping in any one of these buildings.

My phone rang as I was stopped in front of a giant Statue of Liberty, so close you could almost walk right up to it. It was my mother. I sent it to voice mail. It rang again. It was my sister. I was sure my mother was some-where nearby, but I picked it up anyway. I knew Jenny would never hand over the phone to my mother. She would rather dangle it in front of her that she was the only one who could get through to me. I decided to make her day.

"Where you at?" she said. She was always tough on the phone now. All of her friends were like that.

"I am driving," I said. Across the street a pregnant woman posed for a picture in front of Lady Liberty with a set of twin toddler boys and a baby in a carriage. Her breasts were enormous. She licked the palms of her hands and smoothed down the hair of her sons, then arranged them on either side of the carriage.

"Duh. Where are you?" said Jenny.

"I cannot tell you. Where are you?"

"I'm in the garage." I pictured her in there, huddling near my dad's fishing poles, and the extra refrigerator my mom used to stash beer. She looked just like I did at her age, everyone said so. You could hold my yearbook photo up to her face and never tell the two apart. We were twins, only years apart. Of course I had just been that girl on Thomas's arm, and she was something special.

"Where is Mom?" I said.

"Inside, having herself a shit fit. I think she's kind of loving all of this though. At least something is *happening* in her life."

I did not like that my mother was enjoying it, but there was nothing I could do about it. I could not turn around now.

"Will you come back?" said Jenny.

"I do not know," I said, and that was the truth. Was it possible I would never see my hometown again?

"I need you."

"When have you ever needed me?" I said. I laughed. Jenny did not laugh back.

I squinted for a second. I pictured her again. She was not wearing any makeup at all and her hair was all around her in a beautiful golden mess. She was squatting on the ground. Her knees were touching her chin. Her eyes were closed. She held the phone with one hand, with the other she traced the shape of a heart on the ground, like she was feeling her way toward love. Air came out of her mouth slowly. She inflated. She deflated.

"Does Mom know?" I said.

"No. Now will you tell me where you are?"

"No," I said. I did not see how her knowing would help her any, even if she felt like she needed a little power right about then.

"Bitch," she said.

"What you don't know can't hurt you," I said. "And you got enough to worry about, sister."

I heard wild laughter, two almost identical voices, high and girlie, and I turned my head. In the backseat of the cab next to me two red-eyed women wearing wigs—one pink and one blue—were laughing so hard they were crying. What was so funny? I wanted to know. They saw me look at them, and they laughed harder.

"Do you know who the dad is, Jenny?"

The million-dollar question. She was the million-dollar question, and I was the $178,000 question.

"It's one of three people," she said. "There was that one guy, and then there was a party the next night that got a little out of hand."

I said nothing. I was terrified for her. This was nothing like the life I had led just a few years before.

"Doesn't matter who it is anyway," she said. "Ain't none of them want it."

"Jenny, do not talk that way."

"What way?"

"Like-you-do-not-know-how-to-talk-better way."

"Will you tell me one thing?" said Jenny.

"Maybe," I said.

"Is it fun out there?" She sounded kind of jealous. I realized for the first time that it should have been her in this car and not me. A little part of me had always admired her for wanting to break free, even though I had never felt the same way. She was the one aching for freedom. "Is it better than here?" I could hear her heart waiting for me. I did not want to break it. I thought hard. Was it fun?

"It is scary," I said. "And it makes me sad to be away from home." The women next to me laughed so hard it started to worry me. Could you die from laughing? Could you use up all your breath?

"It's not a little bit fun?" she said.

I had not thought about it before, but it *was* kind of fun. The not-knowingness of it all freaked me out. But it was like playing a game, too. I felt like every new person I met, every new city I visited, the farther I got away from my past, I would be making a move. The lies, too, were moves. I had not told any big ones yet but I had told a few, and I knew I would have to tell more before all of it was over.

"It is a little fun," I said. "The most fun of all is letting yourself go. When you just decide to do what you want to do and not listen to anyone else at all—"

"Yes," said Jenny. "That's what I wanted to know."

Maybe it was not a good idea to tell her that. Jenny did not need any more help being wild. But it was the truth. I could not tell her where I was or where I was going, but I could tell her one truth.

We whispered goodbyes to each other and I promised to help her when I could. She asked me when I was coming home and I told her to hold tight. I was lying though. I could not face going home. I did not have it in me.

Traffic moved me slowly down the block and I was suddenly tired. My legs and back and ass felt bloated and sore. I thought about pulling into Paris or New York, but I did not feel I belonged there. I did not belong anywhere. This was a false land. But I had to stop somewhere. I could not drive forever. I neared the end of the strip and I had no choice left. I pulled into the driveway of the giant pyramid.

4.

It was dark and cool in the Luxor Hotel, like someone had flipped a switch and made it nighttime, even though there was still at least an hour left till sundown. There were a dozen long lines of people waiting to check into the hotel. I slid in behind someone. I was happy to be standing still for a moment. But then the soft tinkle of the slot machines wormed its way into my head, and I could see already there were too many traps here. Also, I could not shut out the voices around me. I was in a sea of strangers. I saw and heard everything at once.

The couple to the right of me was fighting. Loud. They did not care anymore who heard what. The man leaned in real close to her face and his lips moved fast. He was fat, and his polo shirt stretched tight against his belly, and great bunches of dark hair came out of the top of his shirt.

The woman had nails that were long and red and she pointed one at his face, the curved tip of it coming close to his nose. He moved away from her. "Enough," he said. "Of you and the way you feel." I thought he was just going to take one step, but then he kept on going. He left her standing there with two suitcases. Her mouth was open as she watched him leave. I wondered if they were checking in or out.

The couple to the left of me wore matching blue wind-breakers and blue jeans. I wondered how it made them feel, to match like that. His head was shaved clean and her hair was wound in rows of tight braids close to her head. She was telling him a story about her grandmother worrying about their flight. There was a late-night phone call involved. The grandmother had offered to pray for them, but she would need to know the flight number, the time they were leaving, and the time they were landing. That would help the praying, the woman told the man. Every few seconds he broke into a big laugh and he would rub her shoulder or brush up against her cheek with the back of his hand. His teeth were bright white in the dark of the hotel. He would never get lost in the dark with those teeth. They were excited to be here. I thought they would have a good weekend. I wished them well.

There was a woman in her wedding gown, much older than me, maybe late forties, blond hair swept up and pinned back with pearl-clustered barrettes, who stood still clutching her bouquet, while her husband leaned in at reception toward a clerk. She did not look deliriously happy, like I did on my wedding day. Older brides are just happy to be there, I guess. She looked calm and content. Her lips were tight against each other. She was not breaking out of her home and leaving her parents behind like I had been.

Her parents were there, with her, I noticed. Her father was blind, and her mother was stroking his arm and speaking directly into his ear. They were tiny and old, shrunken versions of the way they used to be. I bet he called her "mother" and she called him "father" and when they slept next to each other, they would turn together perfectly in the night.

I started to cry, missing Thomas's touch in the mornings. I shaded my eyes with my hand. I did not want people to stare. I looked at the ground. My jeans were dirty. I tapped my foot and waited just like everyone else. People went back to their business, the business of having fun. Someone walked by with a cigarette, and my nose ripened with it. I looked down the lines of people. They were thinning out, things were coming to an end. I shuffled forward with my bag, one step closer to a bed, a shower, a door I could close, a room I could call my own.

I turned to my left and saw a woman standing alone with a bag. She said something to herself, but it was more like she was just reminding herself than having a conversation. She looked tough for a moment, even though she was wearing a strapless black dress held up high on her chest, and heels that sparkled with rhinestones. The muscles in her arms wove through them like they were in a race to the finish. A few men standing in a group near the front of the line turned back and looked at her, quick, like they were monkeys. *A woman traveling alone is suspect*, I thought. But she looked like she could take care of herself. All of her was this mix of being beautiful and strong. Her cheeks were drawn high up on her face like there were invisible fingers holding them, and her skin was smooth and pretty and tan, and there was not a freckle or a blemish anywhere on her. She was one hundred percent smooth. But there was this bold nose in the middle of her face that was so wide it almost seemed crushed. I thought of a boxer after too many rounds. Like she had taken it, and was still standing. Then I let my eyes linger on her bright red hair. There was something wrong with the way it lay flat against her shoulders. She rocked back and forth on her heels and it did not move. It was a wig. Was she undercover just like me?

The line moved forward again. So far I had spent most of my time in Las Vegas in line. It was a wonder anyone had any fun here at all. It was supposed to be so hilarious and nutty and wild, but it seemed like all people did was just stand around waiting for something to happen, or they were walking on their way to somewhere else.

At last a clerk motioned me forward. His hair was shiny, but thinning, and there was a hole in his ear where an earring used to be. He wore a name tag that said his name was Rico and he was originally from San Diego. That seemed like a lot of information to be giving out to a complete stranger. I did not know if I trusted him like he trusted me. I felt uneasy giving him my name. It was all jumbled up in my head, which name I should pick. Was I Moonie? Was I Catherine? Was I someone else entirely? Finally, I gave him my maiden name. I waited to tell him a little bit too long. He looked at me and blinked a few times. Then he asked me for a credit card.

"I can pay in cash, right?" I said.

"Yes, it's just for incidentals," he said.

He typed on his computer. We were both silent. The woman in the red wig was giggling with the clerk two booths over. "I know—can you believe it?" she said. I strained to hear more but I could not.

"The hotel is almost fully booked," said the clerk. He had no accent. He was flat. He could have been from my hometown. I bet he wasn't even from San Diego. "What with it being the holiday season." I looked at him. His face was tan, but the tan could not hide the pockmarks. He was so put together, but so ruined, too. "Most people plan ahead." Now I realized he was trying to make me feel bad, or stupid at least. He was putting me down so I would accept what he would have to say to me. "All we have re- maining are suites." He tapped at his computer. "The starting rate is at five hundred twenty-nine a night."

"Whoa," I said. That was more than the month's rent I paid to live over Timber's diner. Even though I had all that money in the suitcase I was holding, I did not feel quite right spending it.

"That's the best we can do. I can't imagine there's any- where else in town with much that's cheaper." And then he stopped talking because he had nothing else to say to me unless I was ready to pay $529 a night.

"Well . . ." I said. I was stumped.

"I can assure you the suites are quite nice," said Rico. "Or you could always drive to the airport. There might be rooms there."

I did not want to drive anywhere ever again, was how I was feeling. So that is how I ended up staying in the most gorgeous room I had ever seen in my entire life.

THOMAS WOULD HAVE LOVED THIS ROOM, that was the first thing I thought, of course. Two days away from town, three months away from our separation, and still I was running anything new through some sort of Thomas filter. I tried to turn him off in my head every damn day. But I knew him so well; it was hard not to look at things like he would. I pictured him walking through each room— there were four of them, a living room with a kitchen attached, a bedroom, and a walk-in closet as big as the bedroom, and a bathroom with a bathtub for two—lifting up the pillows and sniffing them, pounding his fist on the bed, turning each available switch off and on, the lights, the ones that opened the curtains, the Jacuzzi jets on the pool, which whirred helplessly without water to churn, until finally he settled on the couch in the living room, remote control in hand, flipping the channels looking for porn.

"That's a brand-new flat screen," he would have said. "Not as nice as ours but it'll do."

And I would have said, "The one in the bedroom's bigger."

"You think? Looks about the same to me," he would say. "Should we go check it out? You hinting at the bedroom because you're trying to lure me in there, Mrs. Madison?"

"Maybe I am or maybe I am."

I threw myself on the bed. The mattress bent with me gently at the same time. The comforter was like a mattress all on its own, it was so thick and plush. I took the remote control from the bedside and turned on the television set to a movie channel.

Bruce Willis saving the day, a movie I had seen as a child, one that I was not supposed to watch at the time but did anyway. He talked like he had a cigar in his mouth. There was an explosion—a car turned around and over in the night sky before crashing down below on a shimmery highway—and I shut my eyes, and I saw the explosion behind my eyes, and then I slept.

When I woke it was two hours later, and it was dark outside, but the lights of the city kept my room bright, like a gigantic night-light. The city that never sleeps, I thought. Or was that New York? What was Las Vegas? What happens here, stays here. Where else would it go? Bruce Willis was gone from the television set, but there was Rio De-Carlo, an old movie, one of her first, when she was still up on the big screen instead of making TV movies of the week. God, she was gorgeous. Her lips were real then, real and lush, and these sweet little dark bangs framed her face, so all I could do was stare right into her eyes. She was someone's high school girlfriend in this one. Her boyfriend went off to military school and that is where the trouble started. If I remembered right, she wept at his grave at the end of the film.

I lay right there, still, hands flat against the bed, back perfectly flat, jaw soft, thighs and calves pressed into the bed. I watched Rio hug the boyfriend from behind as he leaned over a trunk he had just packed. They seemed frozen. It was easier that way, to not move. I did not want to leave that room.

I could not turn myself into stone, though, however much I tried. There was blood rushing through me and a bruised heart and an empty stomach that made noises like a monster. My stomach yowled, angry I had let it go to pot those past few days. I went to the bathroom and dropped my robe. I got into the shower. The water pressure was so strong. It pushed up against me and I flattened myself against the wall of the shower. The water beat down on me like some sort of penance or reward. I dropped to my knees and worshipped it. Holy Jesus, was this a nice shower. I scrubbed expensive shampoo that smelled like mint into my hair. I washed myself with honey soap, my breasts and legs and face. I was clean.

I got ready in no time. I wore my favorite short denim skirt and a tight tank top and flip-flops. It was nice to pretend it was summer again. I looked at myself in the mirror while I dragged a comb through my long clumps

of hair. The bones below my neck stuck out like a picked-
over chicken wing. Once I was pretty. I would be again
someday.

DOWNSTAIRS THERE WERE the same lines as before at reception, the same endless flow of traffic, people carrying
drinks or luggage or babies ready to rest. I had never seen
so many people in my entire life. It made my heart beat
faster. My hotel room had made me feel calm, but now I
was just like everyone else again. I stepped into the rush
of traffic and started walking. I did not know what I was
looking for. There were too many places to go and everything forced you to walk through a maze of casino. I need
a bar, I thought. I veered off the path of slot machines, up
some stairs to a gloomy cocktail lounge. There was a long
line of video poker games installed in the bar. It was impossible to avoid them. There were traps everywhere. I sat
at the bar and ordered a beer. After the first sip I felt
drunk. I knew then it would be a long night.

The bartender was named Phillip and he was from
Tampa and his teeth were big and yellow, but everything
else about him seemed quiet. I watched him move down
the bar, serving people quick, and then leaning back
against the same spot on the wall. Nothing seemed to
move about him except for his hands and it was as if his
feet were on some imaginary dance floor behind the bar.

I drank that beer right quick and it felt good.

When I was done I put a five-dollar bill into the video poker machine. I quickly lost it. I ordered another beer, but Phillip waved my money away.

"You play, you drink for free," said Phillip. I felt myself being sucked in. I let the city suck me. I put in another twenty, ordered another beer.

"You like those better than the slots?" I heard someone say. It was the woman who had been standing in line, the muscled woman in the red wig. She had on a blond wig now. She changed wigs just for fun, I thought. She had a funny idea of fun, although maybe I would like it, too. She had changed her dress, too. It was blue and had sparkles across the top of it. It looked nice with her eyes—it was hard to tell in the darkness of the casino, but I thought maybe they were violet, and I had never seen eyes that color. Her eyes were so pretty it made you forget about her nose. And anyway I was starting to like her nose; I could see how it fit in well with all of her, her tough muscles and big breasts and firm voice. And I liked the way her face was powdered and smooth, and the little diamond drop earrings that hung from her ears. She looked really classy. There I was thinking I was looking good in my denim skirt and tank top, and she had just shot herself through the roof of the pyramid. I pictured little stars falling all around her.

"I don't know if I like either that much," I said. "It's my first time here."

"Slots are way better," she said. "You can win bigger. This is just for passing the time."

"You think that's true?" I said.

"I know it is. Once I won five thousand dollars on the slots." She picked up a glass of champagne that sat in front of her on the bar and swirled it. Then she downed it. "And my mother won ten thousand dollars last year. We've got a lucky family."

"You *are* lucky," I said.

"It's in my blood," she said. She ran a hand across the bare part of her chest. There were light bluish-purple veins running across her. Her nails were clean, but they were bitten down to her fingertips, the skin peeking over the tops of the nails like little sunrises. She said her name was Valka, and I said I was Cathy. It sounded like a nice, normal girl name. A girl to pal around with. Definitely not a girl running from her ex-husband with a suitcase full of cash.

We shook hands like we were equals. I knew right then she saw me as just like her. We could be friends. She had more makeup on and prettier clothes but we were both women alone, in the same bar in Las Vegas. She did not know anything about my past, and I did not know anything about hers. I felt myself unwind the tight spot down deep in me just a little bit. We were strangers. Maybe we could be free with each other. I let Valka lead the way.

5.

I began to love the ringing of the slot machines. The gentle repeat made me feel comfortable and safe. Valka and I favored the *Wheel of Fortune* slots. Every once in a while we—or someone near us—would hit a bonus spin, and the machine would play the *Wheel of Fortune* crowd shout from the beginning of the show, and Valka and I would say it along with the machine and giggle. Then we would both stop and look to see if whoever had hit the bonus round was making big bucks. Someone had won five hundred bucks so far, that was it, the rest of them just picked up twenty bucks here and there. "No luck," Valka would mumble under her breath. Then we would order another cocktail. I lost count of how many times we had another round of drinks.

Valka was here to see the Hot Stars in the City show,

she was telling me. She and her ex—Peter Dingle, was his name, no one ever called him anything but both names together, she said—used to come here all the time to see it. For years, they had driven from Santa Monica for a nice weekend of drinking, slots, and celebrity impersonators. Valka's favorites were the Beatles. I was too young to know much about them besides that one Beatle being married to the lady with the fake leg from the motorcycle accident. The dim lights of the casino hid Valka's age from me, but it turned out she was a lot older than I thought.

"My mother saw them on the Ed Sullivan show," she said. She sipped her Bloody Mary, pulpy bits of tomato sticking to the side of the glass. "And she loved them and used to play them for me all the time. But I didn't love them like she did. Like I liked them fine. Catchy songs, whatever. But she was crazy about them. And then one day, I think I was like thirteen or something, I stayed home sick from school. Or maybe it was rainy out, I don't remember exactly. But I was bored and just laying around on the couch, I remember that. And my mom threw this tape of *A Hard Day's Night* at me and I was just that bored, to watch something my mom thought was cool. There was this scene at the very beginning where they're running, all of these fans are chasing them, these teenage girls just screaming for them, and there was something about that moment, the looks on their faces, the way they were all just having a good time, it reminded me of me and my friends. They were so young and free. And I just fell for them. Head. Over. Heels."

I tried to think of one thing my mother had taught me to love that I had taken to but then I realized there was not anything she liked in our hometown. Everything she fantasized about was somewhere else. Europe. New York. Tiny snails and fish eggs you were supposed to eat like they were delicious and not just snobby. They were all things out of my reach. Why would I care? There was not a thing I was crazy about except maybe my husband.

But you could live anywhere and like the Beatles. After she watched that movie, Valka and her mother would sing their songs to each other all day long. "My mother liked all the layers of 'Sgt. Pepper's Lonely Hearts Club Band.' It was like all extreme and complicated. But they don't play that at the show; they play the sweet stuff, their early pop songs. Real crowd pleasers." I had no idea what she was talking about but I was excited to see them. "She loves you, yeah, yeah, yeah," she sang. She drummed her hands on her lap. She stopped being a lady in a nice dress for a second. She was a kid. She told me Peter Dingle had grown up loving the rock-and-roll life back East. (It was neat the way Valka said "back East" so casually, like it was a real place to her in her head.) Bon Jovi was one of his favorites from the show, but he liked all the imitation heavy metal acts, too.

"There's an Ozzy Osbourne imitator who rips the head off a bird with his teeth," said Valka.

"That's not legal," I said.

"Legal or not, it looks real to me," said Valka. She took

a sip of her rum and Diet Coke and raised her eyebrows. "Looks as real as you sitting here before me."

"It sounds like a great show," I said. "I'd like to see that."

"I was hoping you'd say that," she said. "Because I have an extra ticket for tomorrow night. So what do you say? You want to be my New Year's Eve date?"

I was touched like I had not been in a while. Here she was, knowing me only for a few hours, and she was handing over a golden ticket to me. Sure we got along like gangbusters, but still I found myself welling up a bit.

"That is just the sweetest thing ever," I said. "What do I wear?"

"I'll loan you something!" she said.

We drank all night, and I felt the hangover before it was over. I did not mind it. I was caught up in the magic of Vegas. We had spent the night walking from casino to casino, through the crowds of drunks, drunk just like us. It was bitter cold out there, and there was a strong wind blowing, but Valka and I faced it. She loaned me a wrap of hers that matched the one she was carrying. "That's pashmina, you be careful with that now," she said. It was soft, and I cradled it around my arms like I was getting a hug. Oh, how I needed a hug. I stopped Valka on the street and said that to her. She threw her arms around me and said, "Oh, honey, I need one, too. All the time. Every day."

By the time we got to the Bellagio we were a mess. We were spilling drinks and secrets. I tried not to lie too much. I told her my marriage had fallen apart. "It was just the fighting," I said. "We were like two wild dogs fighting over a piece of meat. Our marriage was the meat. Do you know what I mean? The meat!"

"That's not healthy," said Valka. "That's *un*healthy." She thought she had it all figured out now. She had been trying to get the truth out of me for a while.

I held my tongue pretty well, but I was new at having someone to talk to. My secrets still felt important to me. Valka was ready to spill all of hers and I wanted her to feel better. It would make her feel closer to me, to tell her story to me. But then I was afraid I would have to do the same. I was trying to hold off. Telling the truth would hurt. I had been holding onto these secrets so long it almost felt like it all had happened to somebody else. And I would have to reach down pretty far inside to dig them all out. I was not sure if I was ready to do that.

Valka told me the Bellagio was where all the rich men were, but also the women looking for them. "Not that I need anyone else's money," she said. Valka was an independent businesswoman, with her very own flower shop. "I own prom season," she said. "It's mine, and I'd like to see someone take it from me." She straightened her wig and plumped up the top of her dress. "I don't know how to talk to teenagers though. Or kids. Or whatever. I just want to shake them. Prom. Those kids think it's the most important night of their life. I want to tell them there's so much more out there, they have a whole life of mistakes to make ahead of them."

I thought of my own prom, me staring in the bathroom

mirror in the lobby of a Best Western near Lincoln, putting on lipstick. All of the other girls—the girlfriends of Thomas's buddies—were standing next to me in a row, putting on their own makeup. How much mascara did they really need? They applied it so carefully at the beginning of the night; sloppier, boozier, as time went on. Their eyes were sooty clumps by the end, smeared beneath as if they had slept in their makeup. We did everything together the whole night, me and these girls. They would not let me out of their sight. Everyone had to laugh at all the same jokes. Everyone had to comfort Margaret when she started crying about her cousin who accidentally died during the tractor pull last fall. Everyone had to wait in the bathroom when Paula started puking up peppermint schnapps. The room had smelled like Christmas. They were sort of my friends at the time, but I guess not really at all. I did not have many friends then. I had Thomas. I had my mother. I had Jenny. I did not have any friends these days actually, when I really thought about it. Just a lot of secrets instead.

"Let them have their dreams," I said. We clinked our drinks. We were at a bar by then. I had lost three hundred dollars on the slots. I was not lucky, not at all. I had been tempted to lose every last cent of that $178,000 but I knew it was better to keep it safe for now. So Valka was buying everything, and I did not stop her. She was a good friend. We both got wistful, thinking about prom. We could not get out of it.

"I had dreams," said Valka.

"Me too," I said. "I was going to be married forever."

"I almost got married," said Valka. "To Peter Dingle." She looked down at her drink miserably.

It was not going to take much prodding. There was a tiny part of me that still wanted her to hold back. I knew whatever I was going to hear had been said a million times before. It was a real story that had happened to her. I knew she would not lie to me. But it was going to be something she had practiced. And then I thought: maybe she will need to tell it a million times more just to get over it. And secrets were what girlfriends shared with each other. This is how we would become friends. Someday I was going to tell her my whole story. Maybe just some of it. Either way, I would need her to listen.

"What happened with Peter Dingle?" I said.

"Peter Dingle is a fine person," she said. "I should say that. First. It's not his fault he's a *man*."

Oh Lord, I thought. I did not know if I could take a night of man-hating. I liked men just fine.

"Here's what happened," she said. She pointed to her breasts. "It all went downhill from here."

I looked at them. I wondered if they were the best that money could buy. They seemed very impressive: they were at the perfect point in her chest.

"My doctor kept finding lumps in my breasts," she said. "Like every few months there was another lump. All over, both breasts, on the outside, deep inside, all different shapes and sizes. And I was having biopsies every time, and mammograms and sonograms. Everything they could do to a tit they were doing to mine. Needles, wires, the works. And my grandmother had breast cancer, both of them actually. One died young, one's still alive. I had to do these tests to see if I was going to get it. I had the gene. This bad gene. Because I'm Jewish. I have the bad Jew gene."

"This is horrible," I said. "This is a horrible story." I did not want to hear any more secrets. "I'm sorry."

"So the doctor said, 'Chop 'em off and start over,' so that's what I did." She put her hands to the sides of her breasts. "And they're so much better now! Than the way they were. I kind of hated them before actually. They were flat and droopy. They looked like silver dollar pancakes. These look great in anything."

"They're beautiful," I said. I got all hazy for a second. I thought about Thomas touching mine while he looked over my shoulder. I remembered a porn movie playing behind me on the TV set. Imitation and real, all at the same time. Thomas got to have it all.

"And Peter Dingle stuck through it all with me. All those years of surgeries—we were together for four years, and three of them I was in and out of the hospital all the time. He held my hand in the waiting room. He took off work. He helped me pick out what my new breasts were going to look like. He told me everything was going to be okay. He wanted to marry me and have children with me and spend the rest of his life with me and he didn't care what was real and what was fake because he knew what was going on inside of me. That's what mattered to him."

We both started crying.

"I could feel him right here." She clutched her hand to her chest. "He was my heart."

I did not want to hear another word, but she could not stop. And I could not tell her to stop.

"We had the wedding date set. I had my dress. I looked perfect in it. We were going to start all over together. I went back to the doctor for a checkup. I was all clear, my breasts were healthy. But then it turned out there was another spot, but it wasn't on my chest. It was down there." She pointed toward her crotch. "Ovarian cancer. Just like that—" She snapped her fingers. "I had to have a hysterectomy and chemo and the whole works."

I looked at her wig. I wondered how many colors she had.

"I'm all empty inside now," she said.

"You're not," I said.

"And that's what got him. After everything, it was the babies. He wanted his own children. 'This isn't what I signed up for,' is what he told me. 'It isn't what I signed up for either!' is what I told him. He tried to let me down gently, but I fell just like a rock."

I hugged her, and she did not hug me back, and I said, "No, you hug me *now*." I made her hug me. I think she felt better.

"Not his fault he's a man," she said into my shoulder. "That's what they all want, is kids of their own. Men like that."

I pulled apart from her and looked her in the eye. She

was all glassy and drunk. I was, too, but I tried to concentrate. "It's just wrong," I said.

"Oh is it?" said Valka.

WHERE I CAME FROM, people did not drink much, and they sure did not drink till they were crazy. Where I came from, if people drank too much, they got quiet. Sure there were the high school kids running around the fields on a high after the football games. They liked to whoop it up, make a little noise. They were young: they needed to explode sometimes. But they would have been doing that whether or not there was a little nip of something in their thermos or not. Even those parties Jenny went to, the ones that got her in all the trouble, I knew those kids were just making each other warm at night.

And there was my mother, she drank until she got mean, but again, that was already in her. When I was little, she would drink herself so mean she would tell me awful bedtime stories. Jenny, too. It was a special kind of mean between a mother and her daughters. A whispered mean.

Mostly I thought about the farmers, who would drink themselves through the winter. That, or pray. Either way, they got quiet. We were a quiet town. One thing was possible: there was a lot of space between us, between our homes—there was so much land. Maybe if people got noisy I did not hear it. But I do not think so. I lived there my whole life and I think I would have known. If people were losing it, someone would have told me.

There in Las Vegas, though, all people wanted to do was drink until they were someone else. I could not believe all the hooting and hollering. It looked like their faces were melting. People were stumbling, running into walls. I was drunk, too, but I was my daddy's girl when I was drunk: serious with an occasional case of the giggles. Las Vegas did not look like fun at 4 A.M. To me it looked like the end of the world. And Valka, I loved her like a sister already, but I thought maybe she had gone through to the other side. The other side of *what* I cannot rightly tell you, but if she was not already there, she had one foot in the door.

At first I would only have known it from talking to her. There was nothing out of place, not anywhere on her face, not a hair on that blond wig, not a sparkle on the beautiful blue dress. She had been checking her makeup all night. She knew she still looked good. And she did not slur her words either. Valka was making all her points, thinking in complete thoughts, finishing up her sentences. She used words I did not know a few times. The way she was sitting at the bar, back straight, palms flat on the bar, I never would have guessed she had had anything more than a few drinks.

But there was fire in her eyes, I could see it, shooting up toward the rafters of her mind. And even if she sounded like she was making sense, I knew she was going to places that would not be good for her. She was getting loud. It was loud in the casino. But she was getting louder.

The guys next to us at the bar heard Valka talking, and moved a little closer. I thought they were businessmen, with their shaved heads, dress shirts, and slacks, looking all suited up even though it was 4 A.M. Where was the meeting?

"How come you girls aren't smiling?" said one. He wore a thick gold watch that dangled a little loose around his wrist. "Pretty girls like you, there should be some smiles on those faces."

Valka's face collapsed into a frown and then re-formed into a growl.

"You need a drink?" The other one tried to wave down a bartender. He had a hundred-dollar bill folded between a few fingers. "That'll cheer you up."

"Why don't you worry about yourself," said Valka. "About your own personal joy and happiness. Why don't you look deep within and ask yourself, why do I need everyone around me to be smiling all the time? Is there something wrong with my life that I can't deal with reality? Because reality is—"

"You got a fucked-up nose anyway," said the first man, and he and his friend got up and left.

"Whatever, bald asshole," she yelled over her shoulder at him. The bartender came over to our part of the bar and started wiping the counter with a rag and giving us looks like we were trouble. Which we were not.

"We're fine," Valka told the bartender. "Sheesh," she said to me.

"Men. Always wanting you to be something you're

not," I said. I could not believe I had fallen in with the man-hating. Las Vegas, sucking me in again. It is only for one night, I told myself.

We had another drink. Liquor was fifty percent of me by then. I swear it was replacing my blood. I felt darker than ever, and Valka was with me. She was right there. And the ghost of Peter Dingle hovered near us, too.

"It's not bad luck, it's good luck. It's better to know now, you know?"

"That's exactly right," I said.

"What if I had spent the rest of my life with him?"

"Your life is just starting out now," I said. "A new beginning." I was talking about her, but I was the one who needed to hear it.

"What if I had spent the rest of my life with a man with a good job and a nice family and who gave me slow kisses in the morning? That would have been the worst thing *ever*." She spit a little bit.

"He wasn't the right one," I said. "The right one would have stayed."

"I'm going to be alone forever," she said.

"You're not."

"I am."

"I'm not and you're not. Already we've found each other," I said and I meant it.

"You're like my sister," she said. "You and I are like the same person."

We were not the same person, I knew that. And I already had a sister. But there was something we had in common. Our men had left us wrongly. Sure, I had been the one walking out the door, but he had held it open and kicked me headfirst.

"He wasn't that good, you know." She practically yelled the next part. "In bed. Peter Dingle was not so good in bed."

Two guys sitting next to us looked over at Valka when she said that. They had short haircuts, and were not much older than my sister. I thought they were military. I wondered if they had ever killed anyone. That was the way my mind was working. Seeing death in some places. Their gaze was steady on us both, and then one of them said, "Well, just let it out, then."

Then she screamed it. "PETER DINGLE WAS A BAD LAY."

And that was when the bartender asked us to leave.

"I'VE NEVER BEEN kicked out of a bar," I said. We were laughing about it later in bed. "I haven't even really been in that many bars." We had decided Valka should move into my suite and stay with me for the next few nights, at least until I decided whether or not I was going to go with her back to Santa Monica. She said I could help her out with the flower business. She was always looking for someone she could trust. The high school girls robbed her blind all the time, or they were busy on the phone with their friends. The local mothers had to leave early to pick up their kids from school. She was looking for a woman just like her to help her out. Someone she could bring up in the business. Maybe I could be a partner someday, she told me. If I worked hard, took a few classes in business and floral design. There was nothing to it, working in her industry. You just had to have a good eye and be able to think on your feet, and she could see I had both of those qualities. She would teach me everything she knew and then some.

All of this she said to me on the cab ride home, and all of it I agreed to consider. Maybe it was what I needed. A fresh start, a real career, a friend to call my own. Maybe if I kept going, if I pushed west, I could leave the mess I had made back home behind me.

"I get into trouble sometimes," said Valka. "I'm sorry. I shoot my mouth off and I can't stop. That's what you've got to put up with if you know me. Peter Dingle used to love it though. He thought I was the funniest woman he had ever met. Even now when I run into him back home I can make him laugh." She sighed. "I'm just scared I'll never find anyone. I'm too old to start over, and yet here I am, starting over. I was happy having a man to call my own. And now, I have nothing. I am sad." She paused. "Now I am sad."

I loved her so much in that moment. For being able to holler out her feelings. It made me feel better just knowing it was possible.

6.

The next morning Jenny sent me another video of herself. Valka and I were still in bed, laughing about those bald assholes from the night before. I rolled my eyes at Valka before I checked the phone and she said, "Well, if you feel that way about it, don't answer it. There's no pick-up-your-cell-phone law. Especially not in Vegas." She was right, of course, but I could not stop myself from checking. In this video Jenny had her arm in a sling. She mouthed "Mom" at me.

I choked. Thinking again about Mom hovering over the bed when I was a kid. If I fell asleep during her story, she would pinch me to wake me up. Sometimes she would just let her fingers hang close to my arm. Or just move them slowly, so slowly, toward me, while she whispered. I never knew when she was going to strike. That was the worst part. No wonder I rushed into Thomas's arms so quick. He was my steady. I remember seeing bruises on Jenny also, but she went the other way. She craved things out-of-sorts and hectic. Now she was getting it something good. But I was too far away to help.

"Aw, crap," I said.

"What's going on over there?" said Valka.

"Oh, nothing but my family's white trash roots starting to show," I said. I went to the bathroom, locked the door, and called Jenny.

"You would not believe the bathroom I'm in right now," I said when she picked up. I was trying to make things light, to cheer her up. "There's a phone. And a TV. And I think it's made of gold."

"I am so happy for you," said Jenny, but of course she was not. She did not have time for bragging, or any games at all.

"Are you okay?" I said. "Can you handle this?"

"I can't tell," she said. "I can't tell if it was just an accident because we were arguing and she grabbed me the wrong way or if it was for real, and Mom's going crazy and is going to like, stab me in my sleep."

I thought about it for a second. "No, she would not do it while you were sleeping. She would definitely want you to be awake for it."

"That's comforting," she said.

"Well, how else would you get the point?"

We both started laughing, but it was a little moan of a laugh that drained out of our throats quick.

"Call someone," I said. "Go somewhere. Go stay in my old apartment. Timber would let you in."

"I feel like I can handle it," said Jenny. "And anyway we're all snowed in. Dad's completely checked out at this point, and won't dig us out of the driveway."

"Will you just call Timber?"

"If I need to, I will. I'm not that worried though. I'm pretty sure I can take her. She's so lit all the time I probably could knock her over quick."

She laughed, and I strained my ear to see if she was faking it. Oh, I guess I wanted to believe her. I wanted to carry on with what I was doing at that moment. Sitting close to Valka in bed and giggling like real girlfriends. Breaking free from the cold Nebraska winter. On my way to the new me. So I wished her well and made her promise to call me the minute anything happened. But secretly I hoped that phone did not ring. Because I still wanted to have some fun.

Back in bed, Valka gave me her best impression of a worried look, considering her forehead did not move a lick.

"You want to talk about it, Cathy?"

"Nope," I said. "I do not want to talk about anything ever."

Valka took in a deep breath. "All rightie, then," she said.

"Sorry," I said. I instantly regretted it. But I was not ready to spill my soul to the world. I loved Valka but it was so tight inside me. It still hurt to breathe.

Then she said, "Oh well, new day, new year." She paused. "That's right, it is a new year! Tonight, oh tonight.

I am taking you to see the best show on earth, *Hot Stars in the City*. Two lady friends out on the town again. And then at midnight, champagne cocktails!"

"I don't know if my head can handle it."

"You'll be fine. Just take some more aspirin. Or I've got some Valium."

"Valium!" I said.

"I have lots of drugs. I'm a regular old medicine cabinet. I AM A CANCER SURVIVOR." She said it so seriously I could not argue with her.

Valka got up and went to the bathroom and said, "This is magnificent." Then she started puking.

"Are you okay in there?" I said.

"Fine," she said. "Just getting it all out."

"Do you want me to hold your hair?" I said. Isn't that what girlfriends did for each other? That was how it was in high school anyway. Then I remembered she did not have any hair. She did not bother to reply.

I sat back and thought for a moment as Valka retched in the bathroom. She had been through so much. She lost her breasts. She lost her insides. She lost her man. There she was throwing everything up from last night. But still she had a positive attitude. She should have had a heart of stone but she was so much warmer than I would ever be. And I had not even bothered to tell her my secrets. She had not asked, but still, I could have offered something up in the name of friendship. I was the one who was wrong.

Valka turned on the shower and came back into the

bedroom. She was naked. Her breasts really were in a perfect location on her chest. There were tiny pinkish scars on the undersides of them and around the nipples. She opened the closet door and pulled out a robe. "Ooh, these are nice," she said. "They're softer than the robes in my room." She wrapped one around herself and came over to the bed. She sat down on it and faced me. "Do you want to see what I look like without the wig?" She put her hand on top of her head.

I did not want to see it, but I could not figure out how to say no.

"I don't show just everyone," she said.

Okay, it was a bonding thing. I wanted to bond.

"Show me," I said.

She pulled off her wig. Underneath she was still pretty. Her hair was growing back in weird spurts, sure, like there was a strange map of the world on her head. But there were no scars on her head (I do not know why I thought there would be, it was not like she had had brain surgery) and the skin was still smooth. She had washed off her makeup the night before so all that was left was her, just her, just Valka. I put my hand out and touched her head.

"It's fuzzy," I said.

"Soft," she said. "Yes. Sometimes I rub myself for good luck."

We both laughed at that one.

"Not that I need it," she said. "I'm the luckiest girl in the world."

. . .

EIGHT HOURS LATER VALKA AND I were both done up in dresses and waiting in line at the show. I thought she looked prettier than I did. She had brought a special outfit for the occasion, a white dress with red and black rectangles on it, and black stockings with seams running down the back of her thighs. Her wig was puffed up on top, and she wore a wide band across the bangs. The ends of the wig curled up like the edge of a smile.

"Do you get it?" she said to me. "I'm a mod."

I did not know what that was but I told her she looked just perfect, which she did. She looked like she was from another era. If that was what she wanted, to be somewhere else—anywhere else—but here, then I supported it.

I wished I looked as classy. Valka had loaned me one of her party dresses, a strappy gown that swooped down low on the chest, and was shredded at the bottom and covered with sequins so that it looked like my legs were covered with shiny feathers. On her I was sure the dress would look glamorous, but on me it looked like I was trying to grow up fast. Valka helped me tease out my hair and told me I looked like I could be in a Bon Jovi video. "You're a vixen," she said.

I did not want to be a vixen. I did not know what I wanted to be, but a vixen did not seem like the kind of thing that would come natural to me. I missed my flip-flops the minute I slipped on Valka's patent leather high

heels. "They're fuck-me shoes," said Valka. She scared me
sometimes. I stared down and wondered how I was going
to last in them all night, and if I really was required to
have sex with someone when I was wearing them. Maybe
I was a fraud if I wore these shoes. I had been with my
husband for so long. And things had never been right in
that area anyway. I had thought about what it would be
like to have sex with someone else, sure. To see if it could
be better. Or different anyway. But to *fuck*? That was a real
particular kind of act. Fucking was like howling at the
moon, and I was no stray. Or had not been one in my past.
I suddenly wanted to rip the shoes off my feet and throw
them across the room. Who knew there could be so much
trouble with just one pair of shoes?

But there she was, so happy to see me like that, so then
there I was, a rock-and-roll vixen for the night. And later
on we were going to an after-party where all the stars
would be; Valka had found out about it from some fan club
mailing list she was on. She was going to get to meet the
Beatles at last.

But first, the show! Oh, what a show that was! All of
the performers really sounded and looked just like who
they were pretending to be. I thought it would be creepy,
but I really got caught up in it, like everyone around me.
Lots of people were dressed up like me and Valka, like we
all could have been extras in a music video for all the different bands, or in the bands themselves. Even before the
show started it was fun pointing at all the different cos-
tumes, the Elton Johns with crazy disco suits and big sun-

glasses, and Michael Jacksons made up to look like they were zombies from that ancient "Thriller" video, and Dolly Partons, big blondes with big fake inflatable chests (both men and women were dressed as Dolly), and Tina Turners in short skirts and high heels and big spiky wigs. The grossest and weirdest were all the older women dressed up like Cher, wearing these see-through body suits with ribbons covering their private areas just like in that video where she was dancing around on top of a huge boat in front of a bunch of soldiers. There was a huge crowd of them that had all come together. Their bodies bulged in all different directions out of their suits and they were drunk as skunks and cackling loudly. "Icky," said Valka, when I pointed them out. She had become a real lady in that outfit of hers.

And then the show started, and we sat back with some cocktails. What a ride. From the minute the curtain came up, you did not have a moment to think, they would not let you. There were lights and the music coming from the stereo was so loud it was like a fire engine right next to your head. The sets kept changing every time there was a different performer so there was always something new to look at. First there was just an explosion of girl performers all at once: Joan Jett and Pat Benatar and Gwen Stefani and Mariah Carey, all howling out their greatest hits in under three minutes each. The risers looked like city buildings, and they moved up and down when each per-former was beginning. Then the city lights turned out, and all of a sudden there was a sunset with real ripples of water for the Beach Boys, and what looked like real sand, too. "How did they do that?" I said to Valka. I had smelled the ocean, I was sure of it, even though I had never even been to one before.

They all just kept coming, one after the other. All of the performers appeared as their younger selves, as bright young stars—except for Aretha Franklin and Barbra Streisand, they were both older and fat. There was an army of Britney Spearses, all dressed like schoolgirls. Right then my cell phone buzzed, and I looked down at it—it was a video of my sister wearing a stupid New Year's hat, a noisemaker dangling from her frowning lips. Then it was the Beatles. Valka went nuts: she jumped up and hollered, her big headband sliding halfway down her bangs. Valka was not the only Beatles fan. There were a hundred other Valkas in the audience, some dressed like her, more of them hippies, and a few Yoko Onos in the crowd. They were pretty good, I had to admit, even though I did not know much about their music. My dad sang along to their songs when they played on the easy listening station in the car. I suddenly remembered John had been shot. That was all I could recall, that and Paul being married to the one-legged lady. But I could see why the girls had gone crazy for them when they were still a band. Their songs were really catchy and sweet and hopeful, plus the members of the band—the fake band anyway—had cute hair-cuts and big soulful eyes. Valka's voice ran out halfway through their performance, she had been screaming so hard. "I love you," is what she had been saying over and over. "I love you."

At the end of the show Prince came driving out in an actual little red Corvette and the whole crowd shot up from their seats, cheering so loud it was hard to hear the music. Valka's headband fell off completely and she didn't even care. Everyone could agree on that one. We all loved Prince. The entire room of people swayed back and forth to "Purple Rain." Lots of folks had brought lighters and I was jealous because I did not have one. Then Valka reached into her purse and pulled out a few matchbooks from the Bellagio. She was so smart. So we kept lighting match after match and letting them run down to our fingertips. It was dumb but it made us laugh. It was one of the best times of my life. I was grateful to Valka. I could feel myself giving over to the possibility of hope. There was still so much of me that was aching and angry and unwell, but I just wanted to let it go for a second. Just go already.

7.

Later—three drinks later—we were standing in line outside another bar, getting bumped by strangers, though I did not think it was meant to be mean. It was hard to tell. It was like everyone had marbles in their mouth they were so drunk and it was not even midnight. But there we stood in a parking lot, waiting for the celebrity impersonators. It was just a nothing kind of bar from the outside, with mismatched parts where they had added on to it over the years. The bar was sitting right off the end of a strip mall, and we could have gotten Chinese to go if we had wanted, like a few other people in line who were shoveling fried rice into their mouths.

"This is kind of gross," said Valka. "Do you care? I don't care. Do you?"

She was talking real fast. I wondered if she had been

diving into her medicine cabinet. Her purse rattled with all the pill bottles every time she picked it up. But it was okay for her to have a little fun, especially what with what she had been through in her life.

"It is fine," I said. "It has already been a much different night than I ever dreamed I would have. It was like they were all really real."

"They *are* real," Valka insisted. "It was good, right? That show? And now this. Except it's gross. And what if I mess it all up? When I meet them. The Beatles."

I did not know how she could do anything wrong. Even if she did not get along with the Beatles, and got into it with them like she had the night before with those men at the bar, she still would have had her say. I did not know how important it was before I met her. Being heard.

We were not the only ones with the same idea, tracking down the stars of the show. I noticed there were a few Chers farther behind us holding gigantic drinks in fluorescent cups with curly straws coming out the top. They did not stop talking the entire time. I think they might have been from Germany. And right up front, two Mariah Careys, dressed in skimpy little dresses that cut all the way up to the top of their thighs. They looked like hookers, and I said as much to Valka.

"Women are always meanest to other women," said Valka. "My mother told me that once."

"Is that true?" I said. I guess I was being mean for no reason. I did not like that they were first in line, though, and that they were younger than Valka. She was gorgeous but time had already started drawing away the softness of youth from her. She had had a bad year though. It was not her fault.

"But that doesn't mean you're not right," said Valka. "Trash with a capital *T*."

And then came the celebrity impersonators, a dozen of them. They walked to the front of the line. They were in their street clothes, so for a few it was hard to tell who they were. But Prince still looked like Prince with puffed-up hair and pretty cheeks, Tina Turner was still a real knock-out no matter what time of day, and the Beatles—God bless them, I thought—all had the same haircuts in real life as they did onstage.

Valka touched Paul on the shoulder as he passed.

"I really loved the show," she said. "You are seriously the best Paul I have ever seen. Fucking brilliant."

He stopped and turned toward her. He looked at her in her dark wig and rectangle dress, he looked at me in my video vixen dress and my too-much makeup, and he smiled this bashful smile.

"Thanks, love," he said in a British accent. It was not a pretty, dainty one like people usually had in the movies. It was a bit thicker. I held onto Valka's arm. I thought maybe she might pass out. I was feeling a little funny and I did not even care about the Beatles at all. "You coming inside, then?"

"When we can get in there, we will," said Valka.

"Aw, you can get in with me," he said. "We'll take care of you."

We walked up to the front of the line. We nearly floated. I pictured myself for a second flying high above the crowd with the feathers of my dress, the sequins raining down all over everyone.

It cost us one hundred dollars each to get into the bar and Valka paid for both of us before I could say a thing. "You're my date tonight," she whispered. I did not even argue, even though I had $175,000 left sitting in a suitcase in my hotel room. I had seen so much money flying around the past few days I had become numb to it. Money came out one hole and went into another. We were all just trading it back and forth. Mostly forth. It was like they cut you when you got here, a little place in your skin to start bleeding cash. They sucked on you and it felt good. But what happened in the end?

As it turned out I did not really care what happened in the end, because there we were with the Beatles and Bon Jovi and Prince in a table in the back near the pool tables. Paul and John were both paying attention to Valka, who was pinching and looping the end of her wig around her fingers. I was drinking, drinking, drinking. Prince kept going up to the bar and bringing back rounds. Bon Jovi— whose real name was Hugh, and who was from Philadelphia and not New Jersey, but that was close enough for him to be authentic, he guaranteed it—was hitting on me, but only sort of. He had his eye out all over the bar. The girls must go crazy for him. He had the most gorgeous blond hair. Those highlights must have cost a fortune, and I told him so.

"Half highlights, half extensions," he said. "I get it free from work. There's a stylist with the show that used to do movies. He has all these great stories about actresses on crack setting their hair on fire and him having to come in and give them all new hair at five A.M. Guy's a riot." Bon Jovi took a swig of water from a gigantic bottle he had brought in with him. I stared numbly at him.

"You'll never catch me setting my hair on fire," said Bon Jovi. "I'm a professional."

"Do not do it," I said. "That hair is magical."

"I don't do any drugs at all," said Bon Jovi. "Everyone in Vegas is on something though. I hate drugs. Do you do drugs?"

"No," I said.

Bon Jovi put the water bottle to his mouth. It was half full. He drained it. I watched him. It took him a minute, but he did it. Little pearls of water dripped down the side of his face and down his neck.

"Drugs are for losers," he said.

He started to get up, and then he sat down again. He ran his hands through his hair lightly and then scratched the scalp.

"Are you okay?" I said.

"I just need a vacation," he said. He got up again. "I'm gonna hit the head." He walked off into the crowd, pushing his chair over as he left. Everyone at the table looked at me, and I felt all hot.

Prince stood, righted the chair, and then sat down in it.

"Ignore him," said Prince. Prince had a really high

voice and cocoa-colored skin and a penciled-in beauty
mark that was starting to smear. Still, he held himself like
a proud man, sitting up straight, pushing his chest forward
like he was tough or something.

"What's his problem?" I said.

"Oh, no one told you?"

I shook my head.

"He's an asshole."

I laughed and Prince laughed. There we all were, having a good time. *If you could see me now, Thomas. I can
have fun, too.* I missed everyone all of a sudden. I was in a
room full of strangers on New Year's Eve. As much as I
liked Valka, I was missing all kinds of people. If I were at
home I would be . . . what would I be doing?

"Have another shot," said Prince, and he pushed one
toward me. I took it and downed it. "By the way, I really
it like your shoes," he said.

I would be hanging out with my sister and my mother,
I bet. First my mom till midnight, then Jenny would come
straggling in late, stinking of the beer we would all pretend she had not been drinking all night. There would
be an argument, and then my mom would make us all
eggs. Later I would pass out on the couch, feeling together
and apart at the same time.

"And another," said Prince, and he slid me another
drink. I did the shot. I was feeling it in my gut, forget
about my head, that was gone.

"I hate my husband," I said.

"What, honey?" said Prince. He put his hand around

my neck. I looked at Prince. He was so handsome. But also something felt different to me. I stared at him, nodding a bit. Once I started looking I could not stop. He was more beautiful than handsome.

"I hate my husband," I said. "And I took all his money."

"Then I hate him, too," said Prince. "And if you've got all his money, then you're the kind of girl I want to know."

Prince laughed high and squirrelly. I looked at Prince again, at the face and the cheekbones and the little bow on his top lip where the two parts came together. I was not so sure all of a sudden. What he was. If he was a she.

"What are you?" I said.

"What do you mean?" said Prince. Playing dumb. Like my sister when she did something wrong, but she was always doing something wrong so it stopped working. It was not working for Prince either.

"You know what I mean," I said. "Girl or boy? I don't care. It does not matter to me one way or another."

"I'm whatever you want me to be," said Prince. Suddenly Prince had shrunk down. There was no puffed-out chest, just a bunch of delicate limbs arranged together. "But let me guess. You want a boy. It'll be another eighteen months before that's official."

I opened my mouth, but there was no way anything was coming out of it. But I did not really care what he was. I thought about me and Thomas, all of our problems. I could not say anything about anyone else's sex or choices when my own sex life was so messed up. And with my sister knocking around town like she did. Or my mother and father, and the frozen divide between them. At least Prince was interested in figuring out who she really was.

"Have another shot," said Prince.

"I think you should have it," I said. "You're the one who needs it."

"So are you still interested?"

"Interested in what?" I said.

"In, you know, me."

I leaned in close to Prince. "I don't know if there is much inside of me worth anything. I might be broken. I can't feel anything at all." It felt so good to say something so sad. What a relief. This is why people come here, I thought. To tell their secrets to strangers.

"You look like you work just fine to me," said Prince. "You're lovely."

"You're prettier than me," I said. It was true. Prince was prettier than anyone in the room. "It doesn't matter what I look like. Everything is still all messed up in there."

"You know maybe . . ." Prince started stacking all the empty shot glasses on top of each other. Real careful and slow. "Maybe I know things other people don't know. How to make you feel something."

"I'm not that kind of girl," I said. "I'm just, you know, normal."

"How do you know?" said Prince.

I had no good answer one way or the other. But I still

was not going home with Prince on New Year's Eve. Bon Jovi came back and sat with us. He had a fresh bottle of water. Prince got us all glasses of champagne. It was getting closer to midnight. The whole bar was excited about it. Paul and John were both angling to kiss Valka at midnight. I noticed Paul was much younger than John. I was rooting for Paul. He was a real Beatle, being British and all. John was from Chicago. When he spoke he sounded flat, like me. He was still wearing the round glasses he had worn onstage. I wondered who would win out: the sound-alike or the look-alike. Midnight came and I hugged and kissed Prince and Bon Jovi, but just quick pecks on the mouth. I appreciated the way Prince held on to my hair. I let him do it. I let him hold on to me for too long. I did not care what he was. I did not care what I was. I did not care about anything except that Valka had a Beatle for a night. I looked over, and there she was kissing Paul. Her mouth was wide open, almost like she was a fish gasping for air. Every part of her body was attached to his. He had his hands on her breasts, and her back was arched in extreme pleasure. She was feeling all of him and he was feeling all of her. To feel, I thought. To feel deep down. I dug for a second in myself, I imagined my hands reaching inside me, scraping around, but nothing came back up.

We ended up back in my hotel room, the Beatles, Prince, some girls Bon Jovi had picked up, including one of the Mariah Careys. There were a few bottles of champagne. I did not know where they came from. Everyone was talking so much. Bon Jovi and Mariah Carey danced in the corner slowly and licked each other's tongues. There was a knock at the door and there was one of the Britney Spearses, with a bottle of vodka in each hand. "The party's just getting started," she said.

I went into the bedroom and closed the doors. I kicked off my fuck-me shoes and got under the covers, still in my vixen dress. Prince came in to talk to me and sat on the edge of the bed.

"That's a big bed," said Prince. "You got some room for me under those covers?" He crawled on the bed toward me.

"I don't know," I said.

"You're not going to know until you try," he said. He was trying his tricky tricks on me. "I love you, baby," he said. "You know I do." His voice was husky.

He could be anything. He could be anyone. I could be the perfect girl for him. I would never know. Unless I tried.

Right before I closed my eyes I thought of Jenny. It had been a few hours since I had heard from her, but it felt like a very long time.

WHEN I WOKE UP I was alone in bed. My head hurt, but not as bad as I thought it would. I went out into the living room. There was a porn movie playing on the flat-screen TV. That is bad, I thought. Why was that bad? It was registering an alarm in my head. Valka and Paul were asleep on the couch, arms and legs wrapped all around each other. They were mostly clothed. I did not think anything dirty had happened. It did not matter either way. It was her night. The porn, though, that was bad. I could not deal with it then.

I went back to sleep for a few more hours. Then Valka crawled into bed with me and woke me up. She curled up next to me and whispered "Thank you" in my ear.

"You're welcome," I said.

"You know what?" she said.

"What?" I said.

"I never wanted kids anyway. I don't like babies." She slipped my phone around the front of me. "It's been ringing off the hook." I took a look. Ten calls from my mother. It rang again, and it was her. Blinking and ringing.

But then Valka snuggled up next to me and said, "You should just tell her you're alive." Like everything that came out of Valka's mouth, it was the truth. So I hit "talk" on the phone, and let my mother do just that. She had been saving up all her words for a whole week since I'd been gone so they came out in one long line at once, with a little bit of slur around the edges. *It's a little early to be drunk, Mom*, I thought.

"I do not have to tell anyone anything," I said. I rolled over onto my stomach and put my head in the pillow. Valka rubbed my back for me. "I am a single, independent lady," I said.

"Right, a single, independent lady burning up her husband's credit cards at the Luxor Hotel in Las Vegas," she snapped.

Christ almighty, I thought. The porn. It had triggered my credit card. I covered the phone with my hand. "The jig is up," I said to Valka.

"What jig?" said Valka.

Another call was coming in on my phone. It was Thomas. *Finally*.

8.

Been waiting for you to fuck up, little girl," said Thomas straightaway. "And now you done it."

"You are the fuckup," I whispered.

"Having fun?" said Thomas. "Spending my money?"

"Oh, the money," I said. "It is going to be about that. Huh."

"One hundred and seventy-eight thousand dollars is a lot to run off with, Moonie," he said. *Moonie*, oh. I had not heard that in so long. It was so nice to hear it. I hoped he said it some more.

"You got a lot more than that," I said. "Or are you going to hide it under your mattress like your dad did?"

We had never fought very much but we knew how to wind each other up when we did. We were getting ready for something fierce.

"Don't bring my dead father into this."

I apologized, my voice cracking. It was mean. He was dead after all.

"I would have given you money for the rest of your life," he said.

He still loved me. I knew it. I knew he could not let me go.

"But you can't clean me out like that. That is not happening. Not on my watch."

I sank down to the ground. Underneath me someone was getting lucky at a slot machine. Underneath me someone was losing it all at a poker table. Underneath me the casino breathed fake air.

"You're watching porn in *Las Vegas, Nevada,* for Chrissakes. You don't even like porn. Moonie Madison, have you lost your mind?"

I could not argue with him. But I felt the hate burning in me that he was saying it.

"I don't know what you're planning to do but you better stop now. Everyone knows you're crazy. The whole town is talking about you. Stop right now and turn around and come back here with my money and I won't call the cops. It might even be a federal case, Moonie."

I bet he would enjoy that. Men in dark suits driving down dirty back roads to the farm. Maybe they would stop and ask for directions. More tongues wagging. Bet he had been saying "the feds" over and over to anyone who would listen.

He was rambling now, pissed off and out of control. "Just after Christmas, and the bank's calling me all freaked out. I'm just trying to relax with my fiancée during the holidays and now I got this to worry about."

Fiancée. What a joke. He was telling a joke.

I had only been gone a few months. How could he be getting married again? A girlfriend, sure. He did not know how to be alone. He cried when he got lonely. My crybaby husband.

"Everyone knows about you," he said. "Everyone knows you're nutballs. And I am just trying to live my life. Moving on. Like you should be, Moonie."

There is not a single person on the planet who can drive me nuts like my husband. I was hating him and loving him at the same time. We had clawed at each other that last day. The blood and the cruelty, those were the only things left.

"You're getting married?" I said.

"That was fast," said Valka. She sat up.

"That was fast," I said.

"I found a woman to love, and who would love me back one hundred percent and then some."

"You and your money more likely," I said.

"A woman," he said.

Do not do it, I thought. Do not. Do it.

"Who is not a freak of nature inside. Who is a whole woman. A whole body, a whole woman."

"Shut up, Thomas," I said.

"All this time I was thinking it was me, that I wasn't man enough, and it was you. You weren't woman enough, Moonie."

Oh, I was feeling something now. I was feeling something fierce. This was not my fault. A hot bubble of spit in my mouth. I was cursing into the phone. I cannot even repeat it now, the cruel and vile things that came out of me. I will leave it to the imagination. Imagine hate, imagine hurt, imagine humiliation. Imagine months of being alone in your head thinking awful thoughts and then saying it all at once. I was only getting started though. I had so much more to do.

Valka had moved across the room. I was calling my husband a whore, I remember that. It did not make any sense to call him that, but it was how I felt. I wanted someone to strike him down. An evil whore. Valka stood there quietly watching me, her arms at her sides. It was like she had seen a ghost, or maybe she was just seeing me for the first time. She did not know. Nobody knew. Everything I knew was destroyed. I was a tree after a hurricane, roots up. Could she see my roots? At last could she see?

There was me making quiet noises at the end, and crying, and Thomas telling me not to bother using the credit cards, it was all over, they were shut off. I had better get back to town with that money, and fast. And when I got there, I had better be ready to sign divorce papers.

Like I am signing divorce papers, I thought.

"I don't have much use for you anymore," he said. "But I want to get going on this next marriage. There's legal terms for what's wrong with you. I got a lawyer from Omaha and he says he can make it stick."

I could feel my insides crushing, like he had reached in there with his hand and was just squeezing me. My heart was nothing but a bunch of straw to him. I dropped the phone. Valka walked over and turned off the power. She sat and held me as I wept. I was curled as tight as I could be. I was shrinking into myself.

"Tell me," said Valka. "Do you want to tell me? You don't have to. But maybe I can help."

"I need help," I said.

"I will help you," she said. "But you have to tell me the truth."

I looked at her. She was the first person in a long time who did not need a thing from me. She did not need my help, she did not need my sympathy, she did not need my silence. She was pure in her intent.

So I opened my mouth and told her the truth.

Part Two

9.

It started, as most bad ideas did around our home, with a TV show. Thomas and I were watching it on a Sunday afternoon, back home on the couch after our usual breakfast at the diner downstairs: eggs, bacon, white toast buttered on both sides. Our friend from high school, Timber, worked the grill and always waved at me from the rear of the diner. The place was empty. Most of the town was at church. The rest of them would be sleeping off the night before. Sometimes my parents would come and join us, my dad somber and stiff, his handsome face grayed by decades of working indoors, and my mother talking a mile a minute about nothing in particular, secretly mourning the days when she found her life more interesting. I took great comfort in these breakfasts, knowing we would never be like my mother and father. Thomas and I were in love, our marriage was ripe and new, and we did not understand yet that it could be possible to hate each other.

This was when we still lived in town. Before Thomas's father died and left him all that money and we moved back to the farm he had grown up on. Before he had his surgery. Before everything went sour. Thomas had a hand around my neck and he would tickle it when he laughed. I looked at him with love. He had a glint in his green eyes and his baby-soft hair was sticking up in the back, and he was nice and tan from working in the fields all those years. We both had our legs stretched out on the glass coffee table. Underneath, my magazines were stacked neatly by name and by month, the magazines that would tell me how to be a better woman, lover, and wife. The remote control rested between us. It all felt nice, like we were matching parts that together formed one big piece of something. What something, I do not know, but something. It was special, the two of us together. This was when I felt him most, his insides and outsides next to me.

Thomas switched channels like he was shooting off a machine gun. They sped by with hardly a second to know what was playing, but I guess he knew what he was looking for. It was not a sports show, he did not like sports. He had never been able to play any in high school. Some people are not meant for athletics. It was not the news. We had both given up on the news. There were too many wars. Once Thomas had threatened to join the army when we had started a new war. That was years before, right after we graduated from high school, a few months before we got married. "I should sign up," he said. "Serve my country. Do my time." I did not even want him to go down to the recruiting office. I was worried they would laugh at him when he walked in the door. It is not going to make you taller, I thought. There is nothing you can do to make you a bigger man than you already are.

I saw flashes of color while he flipped, the peach of a swatch of skin, the turquoise of a gigantic swimming pool, the almost-white of a perfect beach, the green of a stack of twenties (or maybe they were fifties), and on and on, like playing the slots at the casino, only it was in your head. There were little matching blips of sounds: music and conversation and laughter. Screams and moans and yells. The TV rolled onward, and I just sat there with my legs stretched out, and let Thomas barrel on. It went on like this for a while, I can't say how long. Five minutes? Ten? I looked at Thomas, and he had a grim set to his face. I could tell he was clenching his teeth, and his lips were puckered together. His eyes were holed out, and his eyebrows stuck out in long sprouts near the center. Right then I began to feel separate from him, and I put my hand on his arm and quietly said his name. He did not hear me, he could not hear anything. I said his name louder, and I told him to stop.

"Huh?" he said. He sounded just like he did when I woke him up in the morning to tell him coffee was ready, just the way he liked it. Milk, with lots of sugar. He drank coffee all day long to keep him going.

"Just pick a channel and stay there," I said.

He looked confused.

"It's all the same anyway, right, honey?" I wanted him to know I was not picking a fight.

"Yeah, of course," he said, and he sat up straight and pulled his arm from around me and put it in his lap. He stretched. "I don't know where I went there for a second, Moonie."

I wanted him to put his arm back around me but he did not. He had left me, at least for the moment. He was always leaving and then coming back to me. I scooted closer to him and put my head on his shoulder, and hoped my hair felt nice on his neck, and that the scent of it would drift up to his nose.

I turned my head to the TV. It was one of those make-over shows: extreme, incredible, outrageous. People were always getting new body parts, or moving them around from one end of their body to the other. Injections of flesh, or sometimes there was a giant sucking sound.

The show host appeared. It was Rio DeCarlo, in a bathing suit. She stretched her hands in the air and her whole body stretched with her, her suctioned stomach, her poked-out ribs, the low tide of flesh on her hips. She welcomed us to the show.

"I used to have such a boner for Rio DeCarlo," said Thomas. "Look at her now. Ain't nothing real on her. I like my woman all natural, thank you very much."

That was right, he did not even like it when I wore makeup. "Stay real," he always said to me.

"I guess she got old," he said. He put his head on his hand and puffed his lower lip out under his upper lip.

"She is not even that old," I said.

There was a shot of a man lying in bed in a T-shirt and boxer shorts, above the covers, arms above his head. He was a little older than Thomas and me, and he looked sad. He had pretty green eyes with long eyelashes, and his hair was cut short, not even an inch above his scalp, like he was ready to go off to war. "I have a lot to offer a woman," he said. "But I'm still missing the most important thing." He unfolded his hands and one traveled down to his boxers. He lifted up the waistband and peered down his shorts. "Yup," he said. The screen froze him. He was captured forever looking down his shorts sadly, and then Rio's voice came on: "Today Larry Stoneman will be having penile enlargement surgery."

Thomas's jaw dropped. "Moonie——" He pointed at the screen. "Moonie, watch."

"I'm watching," I said. I pulled away from him, just a scootch, but I hoped he noticed.

"The wonders of modern technology," he said, and I could tell he was truly amazed. "This is it. This is what I need. This is me."

Thomas Madison was a small man in many ways, but still I loved him. He was short, just sixty-five inches high (we said sixty-five inches because it sounded more impressive than five-foot-five), and his arms and legs dangled from his body like a puppet held up by strings.

And he was short between his legs, too. His penis was just a little nub, three inches, if that. Thomas had measured it before but I ignored him when he did it, which was usually when we were in bed together. He stalked into the bedroom, ruler in hand, shutting the door behind him noisily, and then he would jump into bed. This was after he had gone on some sort of quick-growth plan, usually some new vitamin system he picked up at the health food store in Lincoln. After thirty days, it was time to measure. All I knew was I did not want to be there when it happened, so it was: I have to go to the bathroom, I have to call my mother, Did you close the windows on the back balcony because it sure looks like rain out there. I would wait it out for a few minutes out back until I would hear something, usually a sigh of disappointment.

I remember once waiting outside another minute after that sigh, instead of rushing to my gloomy husband. I heard the back door open at the diner down below, and saw that it was Timber. Depending on the day of the week, it was either Timber or the man he switched off shifts with, an older Mexican man everyone called Papi. He and Timber got along great. They went to the movie theater across the street together on Sunday nights after the restaurant closed early. They saw the same movie over and over again, they did not care. It was their one night they could hang out.

I leaned over the balcony and said, "Evening, sir."

"Mrs. Madison," he said, and tipped his hand at me.

"What's looking good today?" I said.

"Why, everything, ma'am," he said.

And then we both laughed, even though I did not know what was so funny about it, maybe just that I was up so high, and he was down below, and we used to sit right next to each other in algebra class, not too long ago. We were playing at our grown-up lives, even though there was not much difference between now and then. We were still there, in the same town, just different locations.

Timber's folks owned the restaurant, and one day he would take it over. He had done his time in the military and then gone to school in Iowa for a year but had been drinking too much, so he came back. Now he was taking night courses in business over in Lincoln and starting from the ground up, back in the kitchen.

I appreciated that small exchange between Timber and myself while my husband measured his tiny penis in the bedroom. I forgot for a moment what was going on in there, that the man I loved was so dissatisfied with himself. I had been numbing myself for years against his pain. It was something I was good at. I had been doing it for so long, what with my mother always squawking like a wounded bird herself. I numbed myself on everyone else's behalf.

I had even tried to get him off the Internet, all those terrible e-mails in his spam folder talking about things he could do to make himself a bigger man. Every time he got online, he ended up in tears afterward. I said, *What do you need a computer for? You're a farmer.* He said, "You're right, Moonpie, the Internet rots your brain anyway." And then I bought him an Xbox for Christmas.

I did not care about size! I told him that a million times. I loved our sex. I loved the way he kissed me, the way he would lick and bite my lips, turning a million nerve endings into molten gold. He would pinch my nipples and the flesh around my hips and press his hands on my belly. The sticky sweet would start to churn inside me and then spread down and around me. I could even smell it, and so could Thomas, and he would get excited by the smell, his little nub would press up against my leg, like a skipping stone in a pocket. He would kiss all the parts of me he had just pinched and then he would keep on kissing, on the bones that stuck out of me, on the insides of my thighs. "Oh, I can smell you, you smell so good," he would say, and he was frenzied then, and warm. The temperature on his hands shot up and I would wonder if he would leave behind burn marks on my skin, an imprint of his fingertips on my flesh forever. I would not mind that, as long as they were his.

"Moonie, my moon," he would say, and then he would dive into the wetness with his tongue, and it was electric. It did, it felt that way, like he had just plugged me into something. And then there were ripples of everything, every area he had pinched and licked on the outside came alive, like he had left a trail of dynamite behind my body, and with one lick, he could set it on fire. Me and Thomas, parts fitting together, moon and stars in one big sky. And by the time he was ready to slide his penis inside me, him letting out a long, satisfied sigh, the breath coming out blowing back my hair from my face, I did not care that I could not feel a thing. A slight pressure around the thighs, but that was just from the weight of him on top of me. But nothing else. I clenched, and then I was numb. And he knew it, too, that it was just numb in there. And I did not care, but he did.

"Night, Timber," I said.

Timber slammed the lid shut on the garbage can. "You take care," he said.

Up above I could see the Milky Way. Inside, my husband rubbed his fingers against the lids of his eyes until he saw stars.

DURING THE COMMERCIAL BREAK we watched an advertisement for the Helping Hand Centers, a chain of plastic surgery hospitals expanding that very moment to a city near you. Rio DeCarlo was their national spokesperson. I did not like the way the name made it sound like a charity. I was sure there was nothing free about it.

"That Rio DeCarlo will do anything for a quick buck," I said.

At the end of the commercial a list of new branches flashed on the screen. "Please don't let it be Omaha, please don't let it be Omaha," I silently prayed.

"Moonie, look! Omaha!"

It was a good thing we did not have any money, I thought. I worked part-time afternoons as a bookkeeper at a welding company with a sinking business supplying various parts to farms across the states. A lot of bigger farms had gobbled up the littler ones, so there was less need for the small-time parts companies. There was almost no point in the job—I made just enough to pay our rent—except I needed the benefits and could keep Thomas on my plan while he figured out what he wanted to do next. He had been working with his father on his farm but they had fallen out the previous year. Thomas's father was a difficult man, neither a saint nor a sinner, just a crank who was never satisfied with anything his son did. Thomas worked the fields and worked them just as he was raised, but somehow it was never fast enough. Farmers were always rushing in the spring when it was time to plant, to make sure they got the crops in before the rain. And rushing in the fall during harvest, bringing in their crops to make their money for the year. I always laughed when I saw how fast Thomas drove during those seasons, and how he slowed down to a crawl during summer and winter. It was like he was two different men during the year, or two different drivers anyway. You could tell what time of year it was by how fast the cars moved on the road. I swear Thomas dropped forty miles an hour off his internal speed limit come November.

That past September, something happened in the field between them. Thomas never gave me the full details. He just brushed me away when I asked him, like I was a mosquito dive-bombing him at dusk, and then stalked off to the balcony to have a chew. "Same bullshit as usual, Moonie!" is all he said later on in bed—but I think it had something to do with what time he got to work. And I was in charge of the wake-up calls in our household. I had been sliding lately when it happened. I had my own seasons, too, as a farmer's wife, and it was always like that at the end of summer with me. I wanted to sleep in, snuggle up next to my husband. Thomas said he did not mind, he never blamed me for a thing, he liked being close to me in the mornings, too. Still, I was afraid to push him as to the whys and what-fors of the fight. We squeezed as much as we could out of his savings and I let my mother slip me some cash here and there, until he figured out his next move. "All's I know is, I never want to work another farm again," he said. But what else do you know how to do? I thought. His unemployment killed any notion of having a baby, but Thomas was in no rush to have kids anyway. He saw all our high school classmates getting married and stacking up babies like pancakes in the morning. Filling themselves up with these new lives, is what I thought. Thomas said they were giving up their free time, giving up their peace and quiet. "I don't want to share you with anyone," is what he would tell me. I would not have minded a little one running around the house, but I could not argue when we did not have much money anyway. There were a few months in there I was hoping he would start college, like Timber, but I was not going to push. For now, we lived our unconventional life, me supporting my man.

So I had no fear as we watched the commercial for the Helping Hand Center, only a low-grade buzz of annoyance. It was like his pill diets, or that time he ordered a box of ginseng online and he sipped it in tea for six weeks straight, or when he hung that weight off it for an hour every night (*that* he learned about from some show on ancient African tribes on the National Geographic channel). It was an idea that would flit and float around his brain like a bird until the season changed, and it was time to head somewhere new. I was the only thing that had ever stuck with him, and that was the way I liked it.

And then a week later his father died on the front porch of his house, sitting and watching the sun set with his dog sitting next to him. Alone in death, just him and his dog. (He had chased Thomas's mother away years before; she lived in Iowa City with a new husband and a Guatemalan baby girl they had adopted our senior year of high school.) His father had an aneurysm. The doctor said there had been all this pressure building up in his brain for a while, maybe even for a year, and that could have been why he had been more difficult than usual. It was one of those things you can't track or test, it just swells up like a balloon. Then it is like someone took a little pin and stuck it in your head and it explodes.

Three days after the funeral there was a call from the lawyer. Thomas's dad had left him everything, the entire farm, and all of the money he had been stashing away for years. He had not been spending it on anything but build- ing a bigger farm, a bigger legacy for his son. Here Thomas was thinking he could escape it, but there it was, more money than we could have ever dreamed of, and land, acres and acres for the taking. It was like we had won the lottery or something, only someone died. It was more money than we should have had. It was more money than we deserved. It was where our problems began.

"AND NOW," I said to Valka, as she cradled my head in her lap, "I want it to end."

We were curled up on the bed. My eyelids were swollen tight and I could only see a sliver of the room. My voice was raw. I had screamed too much. I had not stopped talk- ing for an hour straight. Valka stroked my hair, all the way to the end, all the way down me, head to waist.

"We can make it end," she said. "We can make any- thing happen."

I almost believed her.

10.

What did I know about sex anyway? What does anyone know about it? I was only ever with the same person my entire life, so what we made together was what I knew as right. I read the magazines. There was too much detail in some of them, outright lies in others. Be aggressive toward your man. Be a pleaser. Nibble. Grip tight. Tickle. Or: wait for him. Let him lead the way. But I ask you, what did he know either?

I watched the movies, too. Movies made just for girls who lived nowhere near Nebraska. Saucy language, bold women. Inside jokes I got only half the time, two minutes later than I was supposed to. Those girls had a different life than mine. They were busy looking in the mirror, changing into another outfit. They were waiting for their man to say something witty, or trying to beat him to the punch. They did not know about being turned on by the smell of earth and hard work on their husband at the end of the day.

I watched the movies Thomas liked, too, the dirty ones. From standing to screwing in no time flat. I hated the high-pitched squeals from those girls with the ginormous fake breasts, bouncing up so high I wanted to yell, "Duck!" at the screen. Thomas loved those movies. Thomas, who never wanted me to wear makeup. Thomas, who said I should keep my hair long, and never change the color. "Keep it real," he would tell me. Thomas watched those movies sometimes when I was not around. All I could wonder was, why am I not enough for him?

There were the other girls from town—I guess I could have talked to them about sex. It seemed like that was all they wanted to talk about when I was growing up. There was a slumber party I went to in high school, a few months after Thomas and I did it for the first time. We played a game of "I never" that I ended up losing, or winning, depending on how you looked at it. (Rim jobs? Oh dear Lord, I almost passed out.) Then Margaret kept talking about how big her boyfriend's penis was, calling it practically every name in the world but that. I think she had even made a few up. "I love sex," she said. "Call me a slut, but I love his big ol' ding-dong." She made all the other girls spread their index fingers apart to show how big their boyfriends' penises were, then offered her opinion. "Five inches, that's average, that's what they say," she would say and nod. I froze, then lied and said I was still a virgin.

Everything they were talking about, the way it felt inside of them, the length, the girth, none of that was familiar to me. I was hoping some of them were lying, too. I locked myself in the bathroom later and cried and then pretended I had puked when they started knocking on the door. I never went to another slumber party again.

And then there was my mother, who told me too little, except sometimes when she told me too much. There were the bedtime stories that scared me. And once, when I was fourteen years old, she took me for a walk around the block at sunset to talk about sex.

She was being as honest as she could, I know that now, but she was being something else, too. This was a few months before I started high school, before I met the boy who would become my husband. I was just a little sprite of a thing, but I had long blond hair that fell down to my waist in long waves. It was almost like she could see it coming before it happened and she wanted to get her digs in there first, before she lost me for good.

Our block was noisy on summer nights. There were kids all around, hollering, tweeting, screeching, and they played stickball till sunset and then raced after fireflies with nets and mason jars until their mothers called them home. Jenny was doing cartwheels for our father on the front lawn. Off in the distance, past the bowling alley and down the back roads, the cornfields washed back and forth quietly in the wind. Not that I could see them, but still I knew they were there. I had an ice cream cone in one hand and it was a sticky mess. My mother had bribed me out

the door with it. Her breath was thick with cigarettes
and the smell of that wine she drank out of a giant box
near the kitchen sink. This was before she started drinking
beer. She said she switched because she never knew how
much she was drinking from that box until it was gone
already. I think she just liked to crush the empty cans with
her fist.

"I'm going to tell you a story, Miss Catherine," said my
mother. Her hair was up high on her head still from her
day at work, her lipstick long gone, dark moons of eye
makeup pooled under her eyes. She was smoking one of
her Virginia Slims. I still thought she was beautiful and
classy. "And I just want you to listen close. Don't ask questions. Just listen."

I had heard parts of the story before in my life. There
were always bits and pieces of it floating around my
brain but it was hard to put it all together. It hurt to put
it all together. Her mother dying when she was still little, her father dying when she was in high school. Cancer everywhere, but still my mother smoked. "I know I
shouldn't," she said, and then she took another drag from
her cigarette. How she met my father at an ice cream
social when they were in college, but she had put their
relationship on hold. She had majored in international
studies, and was supposed to move to France for a few
months. That immersion program that was a disaster. She
got lost on the streets of Paris. Or was it the trains? She
got off the plane and turned right around and came back.
She never even saw the Eiffel Tower, not even from a dis-

tance. Sometimes when she told the story she said she came back for love. (Depending on how she felt about my father that day. Or how much she had had to drink.) He had loved her, she said. Someone had wanted to take her on, take care of her. Her lonely orphan self. My mom could make us feel sorry for her any time of day or night. Maybe we did not like her very much, but we knew she had her pain.

"And now I am going to tell you my one regret in life. I held on for so long. My virginity was a precious thing. Now I know girls these days don't see it that way anymore, but I am telling you it is important. I waited for your father forever. And then, two weeks before we got married, we just could not wait a minute longer." She stopped walking and I stopped with her. There was a ripple in her voice. "Well, *he* couldn't wait. I could have waited."

I did not say a word. I was scared all of a sudden.

"Let me tell you what it's like, Catherine." She moved her face in closer to mine and leered at me. I held my breath and waited for the truth. "Imagine a wall. And imagine something pressing up against that wall as hard as possible. It's like this brick wall, and something's trying to break through it." She flattened one hand in the air and punched it with her other hand. I could feel the punch deep in me. "You are that wall, Catherine. You're the wall."

I dropped my ice cream cone on the ground and did not stoop to pick it up. The ants were all over it in seconds.

I heard those words again in my head, for days and days,

for weeks, for months, for the last ten years, forever, in my head, my mother, her fist, the struggle, the wall, and me.

I did not have sex for a few years. I was in no hurry after that. But it did not matter how long I waited. I was already ruined. Maybe I had been ruined before that. I remembered that, though. Other things she had said about sex in the past floated faintly in the back of my mind. But I remembered that walk around the block.

"YOUR MOTHER SOUNDS like a real piece of work," said Valka.

"It does not matter what she is," I said. "You can't go blaming your parents for your problems forever. What happened was between me and Thomas. Between a man and his wife."

"True, that," said Valka. "You have to own your issues. They are yours and no one else's. But, my dear, darling friend, I am just trying to understand here. Why you can't feel."

"I don't know," I told her. But that was a lie. I had more secrets to tell. It is just that they were not my own.

11.

I did not marry Thomas for his money or his looks. I married him for his heart and his sense of humor, and the way he looked at me and made me feel like I was more precious than gold. But I will say this: it was nice to be rich. First thing Thomas did was hire someone else to run the farm. Thomas would still go out on his tractor because what man doesn't love a tractor? There he was whooping it up all over the farm, cowboy hat on his head, straw in his mouth, little legs dangling over the sides. But the day-to-day stuff he handed off to someone else. "I've got more important things to be thinking about," he said. "Like making my bride happy."

Then Thomas set to fixing us a brand-new home on the land. He tore down the farmhouse he had lived in practically his entire life and brought all of his friends into our home. ("They're the biggest construction company in town," he told me. "They're the only construction company in town," I said.) He bought a satellite dish, and a gigantic plasma flat-screen TV, and a five-piece leather couch, and he put a hot tub in the backyard though we hardly used it. I quit my job. We hung out all day watching television and eating bacon. The construction guys were in and out and around the house every goddamn day banging their tools and blaring the country station and smoking out back in the spot where we would someday have a sundeck. I suspected they sneered at our laziness, but I did not say a thing. I did not mind all of the dust and noise so much, only I wished it were just me and Thomas all the time.

At sunset we would take a walk through the field. He would ask me if there was anything he could do for me.

"What can I buy you? What do you need? What would make my bride's life complete?" he would say.

"Just you," I would say, and then he would hold me and kiss me and then we would go home and watch soft porn on cable and do it on the living room couch.

A FEW MONTHS AFTER the construction started I went to my mother's house for a visit, and when I came back everything had changed all at once.

My mother and I had eaten an entire bag of microwave popcorn and had two cans of beer each. We were both bored. Not working is boring. My dad had gotten a job as the general manager of the Walmart off the interstate in York. There was a picture of him, bald with a gray rise of hair around the base of his head like rings around Saturn, which was framed and posted in the front of the store, next to the picture of the employee of the month. My dad had asked my mom to quit her sales job in Lincoln years back, and even though she loved that job for some reason she had said yes. And I never had to work again if I did not want to, and my husband was busy turning the farm into his playland. So some of us were busy, and some of us were bored.

We had taken to drinking a few times a week in the afternoons, me and my mother. Just a can or two to take the edge off of nothing in particular. Beer just made everything a little funnier. My sister's hickeys racing like a forest fire down her neck. My father's hazy greetings when he came home from work. The way my husband would whimper late at night, sometimes for his father, sometimes for his nub, sometimes just because he was fragile and needed to cry. The fact that I could not feel my husband between my legs. Not that I cared.

It was all so hilarious after two Coors Lights. Even funnier for Mom, because she drank an entire six-pack.

"Oh God, I don't know what I'm going to do with that girl," said my mother.

"I think Jenny's just having fun," I said. "She is a smart girl."

"Smart or not, she's wilder than you ever were. You just wanted to settle in right away with Thomas, and that had its own set of problems, but at least I knew who you were with at night. That girl has a new boyfriend every week." My mother shook her head, tilted her head back, and drained the last of her beer. "I don't know where I went wrong. I gave her the same sex talk I gave you. Nothing can slow her down though."

All of a sudden, I shivered. I wrapped my arms around myself. I felt myself fall down deep inside. There was nothing to stop me, nothing to hold onto. I just kept falling. I was empty in there.

"I have to go home to my husband," I said. I stood up and bumped the table. "He will be waiting for dinner." I pushed the chair back and it fell over. I did not pick it up.

I drove slowly and took the back roads on the way home, the dust from the gravel rising in thick clouds behind me in my rearview mirror. Me and my wake. By the time I pulled into our drive, I had sobered up enough that he would never know a thing. Plus I had chewed some gum. Not that he would care if I was drinking, just that he might worry. I hated it when he worried.

When I walked inside the house, the screen door banged behind me loudly and I felt the split of a headache start in my head. The TV was blaring from the living room, and I was not in the mood, so I headed for the bedroom instead to take a nap. If only I had joined my husband on the couch like usual, instead of leaving him alone with his devices, those goddamn remote controls. There were at least a dozen of them, one for the stereo, one for the satellite, three for the TV, one for the video game, one for the DVD, one for the VCR, one for the DVR—and then a bunch more that I did not recognize. There he was, playing with his toy. I could hear the whirl of him channel surfing, and I put a pillow over my head, until I heard "Honey," loud, and then louder. Then he was standing at the bedroom door, and he said, "Honey, are you sleeping?" He pulled the pillow up from my head and said, "Baby, are you asleep?"

"I was trying," I said.

"I didn't know," he said, and he looked so bashful and silly that I forgave him right away. "Anyway, you should come watch this show with me. That Rio DeCarlo show. Do you remember, we watched it a while back? It's that guy who had the surgery I want to get. They're showing what happened to him after the surgery."

Now it is one he wants to get? Oh boy. I roused myself and he held out his hand and pulled me up from bed and then he led me—dragged me, more like it—to the living room, where the tail end of a diet pill commercial was playing. The "after" version of the woman was beaming on the screen in her old pair of blue jeans, the front of which she stretched out in front of her as if she could not get that part of her past away from her fast and far enough.

Thomas pulled me onto the couch next to him and threw his arm around me. He happily threw his legs up on our coffee table, the new one, bigger and shinier than the last one, though in all other ways, exactly the same. It was as if we had taken our old life and inflated it.

He patted me on the leg and pointed at the screen. "Now watch."

There was our old friend Rio DeCarlo, lips puffed out like a million bees had stung her. I bet she did not feel a thing, though, not one little prick. Those lips had to be numb already. She was wearing a ball gown that shimmered with glittery red stones and a diamond necklace with a giant heart-shaped stone at the end. She moved her hands up in the air again, then swung around for no reason. I thought about the first movie of hers I saw when I was a kid. She played the spunky teenage daughter of the president of the United States, though she was probably in her twenties by that point. She ran away from home and backpacked across America while the FBI and Secret Service chased after her, and we all rooted for her in the theater to keep on running. It made no sense, we were all happy to go home to our parents at night, but in that theater that day, we could see how there was another way that was possible. There was the chance of freedom. She had freckles then. Now she had a nose sculpted like a pencil, two nostrils sticking out like tiny peanuts.

"One year ago, Larry Stoneman had penile enlargement surgery, adding a grand total of three inches to his penis. . . ." Rio DeCarlo hesitated for a moment, and I thought I saw her crack a smile, but maybe I was just imagining things. And then she added, "When erect."

There was a shot of Larry holding a ruler and grinning.

"Let's check in with Larry to see how his surgery has changed his life!"

"For a while I played the field," Larry said.

There were a few scenes of Larry sitting in a bar that had flashing disco lights in the background. There were women surrounding him, girls with their hair blown out straight. They were all smiling and laughing—they were having the best time *ever*—and then they all clinked glasses. I looked at my husband's face and I could see he was impatient. Playing the field was never his thing.

"But finally, I've found the girl of my dreams." There was Larry, with a pretty brunette in a low-cut sweater. Her breasts looked suspiciously like Rio DeCarlo's breasts, carved out and propped high on her chest. They were holding hands in a café. The sun struck down between them and around them and they both laughed. I reached for Thomas's hand and squeezed it. It was nice to see Larry happy.

"I can satisfy her needs," he said. Larry's girlfriend gave a little thumbs-up sign to the camera, and then winked. "And, boy, does she satisfy mine." They were on a beach, in bathing suits, embracing and kissing. Larry's hands were on his girlfriend's ass, which was clad in a thong. So it was basically Larry's hands, cupping her bare ass, on national television.

"That could be us, honey," said Thomas.

"That *is* us," I said. "We're already happy."

"I know you're not. You're lying. You never feel a thing and you know it."

I was quiet for a second. I should never hesitate during an argument with him because then he thought he had won. But I did not want him to say what we both thought sometimes, our shared fear. Maybe I just couldn't feel *him*.

12.

I was always that way," I said to Valka. "Like from the very first time." I had showered and was wrapped in one of the gigantic bathrobes. It was so big my hands had disappeared in the sleeves. "Like first base, second base, when we were kids, that I felt just fine. We went out for a long time before we did it so I guess we did not know it was going to be a problem."

"First base?" said Valka. She poked at me. "That's adorable."

I blushed. "You know what I mean. Anyway, when we finally decided to lose our virginity, it was such a big deal. Huge." I stretched my arms out wide. "We talked about it for months, planning and plotting it. Then I lied to my parents about where I was going to be. Thomas got us a hotel room in Lincoln, downtown at the Cornhusker Hotel, which is super fancy. It has this big spiral staircase and chandeliers in the lobby. I do not know how he did it to this day. I am sure the people who worked there must have been wondering what these kids were doing checking in together but nobody said a thing. Thomas checked us in as Mr. and Mrs. Madison. I was acting like I was a grown woman with my luggage, but I was only sixteen years old. We lit candles and drank beer and I put on a special bra and underpants set I bought at the Victoria's Secret. It was pink with little appliquéd baby roses on it. Really sweet."

"Sometimes they do cute stuff," said Valka. "But I think they're way overpriced."

"I did not really want to do it. I will say that right now. I could have waited forever and a day. But he wanted it. He had wanted it since the day we met. It was like we were husband and wife already, that was what he kept saying. 'We're lucky,' he always told me. 'We skipped all the hard parts and found each other.' I believed him."

"Kids," said Valka. "Always wanting to grow up too fast."

"So there I was, lying in bed in my fancy underpants. I remember him putting the condom on. He was calling me Mrs. Madison. That was all I could hear. He moved around on top of me. And then it was over just like that." I snapped my fingers. "I did not even know it had started."

"Boys go quick when they're young," said Valka.

"But I did not feel *anything*," I said. "I did not even know he was in there. I felt like there was this wall in me, and nothing was going to break through it. It went on like this for months and months. I was so scared. I did not say anything about it. He did not ask how I felt, if I was having a good time or anything. He did not know yet that he was supposed to do that. And I did not know he was supposed to do that either. We were so young. I was so numb. And then one day he asked me if I liked it. Maybe he figured out to ask from a TV show, maybe one of his buddies, I do not know. He could tell I was lying. It all came out then. It was a mess. But it only brought us closer together. Together we were going to figure it out. Because that is what married couples did. It was either that or divorce."

"You were sixteen," said Valka.

"We were married. Or something like it," I said. "We were like one."

A FEW YEARS BACK Thomas had decided we needed a joint solution, and that could only be found in a sex shop. We drove down I-80 for a few hours, just over the Iowa border, where he had heard there was a magazine shop off the interstate that sold all kinds of helpful paraphernalia. Like little extra bits he could strap onto himself, just to give him an extra inch or two. And there were oils and creams and pills for me, to make me more "sensitive" down there. I had protested, but Thomas sweet-talked me into going with him. When we got to the store, I refused to go inside with him though. There were signs up all over the outside of the store that said "Triple XXX" and "Adult Magazines" and "Open 24 Hours," and the windows were covered with curtains and I have never trusted a place that you can't see inside. Plus there were a dozen big rigs sitting outside in the parking lot. It was the middle of summer and I was wearing a short skirt and a tank top and I suddenly felt naked. Thomas cut the engine off and the car immediately flooded with heat, the sun ticking off sweat points on my body.

"I do not care to mix with truckers in a dirty magazine store today, Thomas Madison," I said. I was quiet. I never raised my voice to him. The few times I had he had always cried, and then I ended up doing what he wanted in the first place just to make him feel better. I had learned to keep my voice low and my thoughts clear when I disagreed with him.

"I'm sure that part's separate," he said. "Come on, baby, it's better if we do it together."

"I will not go in there today," I said. "Or ever."

"Fine, I guess I'll have to make the extra effort to make our marriage work by myself," he said. His guilt trip was not going to work. I stayed put, crossing my arms across my chest to make sure he knew I was serious. The tiniest gestures would work on him.

He opened the car door.

"I'm going," he said.

"Go," I said. "And leave me the keys."

"Why do you want me to leave you the keys?"

"Because I want to listen to the radio. Because it is hot and I want to keep the AC going. And because I cannot believe I let you drag me all the way out here, that is how come I want the keys." As soon as I said all that, I felt better. I was hoping I would soon find all of this funny, though I had not yet.

Thomas slid the keys into the ignition and turned on the car, and looked straight ahead out the window, paused, and then said, "You're not going to leave me here, are you?"

"Like I would leave anyone I love in a place like this," I said.

"I'm just going to take a peek," he said.

"Go on, then," I said.

I watched him after he got out of the car and headed to the dirty magazine store, kicking dust and gravel behind him as he walked. I slid over to the edge of my seat and fiddled with the radio until I hit an all-news channel. A famous zoologist had died. He was filming a TV show, something about deep-sea diving, and had bumped into a stingray in the middle of the ocean. The stingray stung him in the chest. Pierced directly into his heart. He died almost instantly. He left behind a wife and child. I remembered I shivered as I listened to this. It was hard not to imagine how that hurt, even if I did not have a child. I did not ever want to be left alone. I turned down the AC and wrapped my arms around myself.

There was a knock at the window, one of the truckers, a red-faced man with small nervous welts around his neck.

His eyes were blue in the center, but yellow and red where the white should be. He asked me to roll down the window. I rolled it down just a tiny bit. His scent was so strong it made it through even just the inch of air between us. I pulled back away from him and started breathing through my mouth.

"Are you working?" he said.

"Working?" I said. "On what?"

"Don't worry," he said. He winked. "I'm not a cop."

I was willing to take crap from my husband, but not strangers who smell like whiskey before noon.

"I do not know what you are implying, but my husband went inside to use the restroom, and he is ginormous and will kick your ass if you do not step away from this car right now, and I will scream, I will . . ." I just kept rattling things off until he mumbled, "My mistake," and drifted off slowly at first toward the hub of rigs, and then he turned and looked at me, at my fierce and determined face, and then he began to hustle toward his truck. He rolled out of the parking lot in less than a minute. Filthy man.

But could I blame him? What was I doing sitting in the parking lot of an adult bookstore on a Tuesday morning? I was going to kill my husband. I rolled up the window and blasted the radio. I pulled a shiny tin package of gum out of my purse, popped a piece in my mouth, and started chewing. I pulled on my jaw like it was the lever of a machine. My knee started twitching up and down. I crossed my arms. A few minutes later another trucker knocked on the window. I stared straight ahead. He knocked again, so

I slammed the back of my hand up against the window, middle finger up in the air. He cursed me, then walked away.

That is it, I thought. I am a married, respectable woman. I will not be cursed by truckers. I put my hand on the horn, and I started pressing it, alternating between long spurts, and short little beats. I did this until the front door of the bookstore opened. A lean man in a white and black striped dress shirt walked out toward our car, loping with his long legs and black cowboy boots. He walked with a purpose, that purpose being to stop me from beeping and destroying his business. He tapped on the window. I rolled it down, again just a short distance. He did not look angry.

"Hon, is there a problem? Are you okay?" He smiled. His teeth were gigantic. There were three wavy lines indented into his forehead. They were so distinct, it seemed like they had been drawn there, like a caveman's drawing on a wall. The symbol for fire, or a river, or the slaughter of an animal.

"Can you send my husband out?" I said. I was chewing my gum really fast. "I really want to go home."

"Who's your husband?"

"Thomas Ma—" I stopped myself. Maybe I should use a fake name, I thought. Last thing I need is our good name getting out. "Just Thomas. Just say, 'Thomas, your wife wants to go home. Right *now*.'"

"Are you sure you don't want to come in and find him yourself?" he said. He leaned in closer to the window and hooked his fingers over the top of it. "You might find something you like inside." He was looking at my little denim skirt, my legs, my strappy tank top, and then my face. He did not see it right, though, I could tell. He did not see it as the skirt I bought at my daddy's Walmart with his employee discount to keep cool in the summer days, but as a short trashy little skirt for a short trashy little girl who hangs out in the parking lot of dirty magazine stores. Even though he did not know anything except that my husband was inside—my husband could be a complete psycho—he still acted as bold as anything. There are certain men who do that, act like it is okay because they are flattering you. It is all in their tone. They think they control the world. They probably do half the time. I am not saying it is right, I am just saying they know how to work things to their advantage.

"Just tell him that his wife is sitting out here waiting for him," I said. I rolled up the window and he snapped his hands back. He put his fingers to his head and gave me a little salute, and then turned on one foot and marched back to the shop. It made me laugh, even though I knew he was a scumbag.

A minute later, Thomas came hurrying out to the car. He was empty-handed, and looked terrified. He got in the car, put it in drive, and pulled out of that trucker hellhole parking lot and onto the freeway.

He was dead quiet until he hit seventy on the interstate.

"Way to embarrass me, Moonie," he said.

"What, in front of all your new friends?" I snapped.

"What about me? Did you know there were truckers coming up to me thinking I was a hooker? They wanted to pay me. To have sex with them."

Thomas looked at me, his jaw dropped, his mouth open wide, and I took my hand and pushed his chin up until his lips met. And then came the waterworks.

"How could I have done that to you, Moonie?" One tear, and then it seemed like there were twenty tears all at once, streaming down his face. He sniffled for a few minutes; I let him get it all out.

"Oh, it is all right," I told him. "There are better ways to spend a Tuesday, but it is not like anything really bad happened."

"That place wasn't right anyway," said Thomas. "I went to hit the can and there was a glory hole in there, swear to God."

"What's a glory hole?" It sounded sort of pretty. I pictured a black hole in the night sky with stars twinkling all around it.

"It's where . . . people put their dicks in them. For sex."

That sounded like just about the most awful thing someone could do. Sex through a hole, where you could not see the other person? Or touch them or kiss them? I did not get it. I puckered my mouth. "And what happens after?" I said.

"I think it's maybe gay. I don't know. Your friend Timber'd probably like it."

"What are you talking about?" I said.

"Everyone knows he's gay," said Thomas.

"He is?" Suddenly I liked Timber a lot more. I did not know why. I guess being gay just made him more interesting.

"That's why he had to leave school. For being gay."

"They can't kick you out of college for being gay," I said. "That's illegal."

"They can kick you out if they catch you sucking your professor's dick."

"Shut up, Thomas," I said. "That is just not true. They would just fire the professor. And, anyway, how would you even hear something like that?"

"I don't know all the exact details, little miss smarty-pants," said Thomas. "I just know I heard it around."

I looked out the window. A sign said we were sixty-five miles from Omaha. We still had a long way to go before we got home.

Thomas tapped his fingers on the steering wheel. "It's sort of funny, huh? All of that with the truckers."

"Not yet it isn't," I said. But eventually it would be something we could laugh about. It was all temporary, a piece of plastic he would have added to himself, so I could temporarily feel him, during a temporary moment, which is all sex was. That was why I did not care that I could not feel him. It was just one part of a lifetime of moments I planned on having with him. And the non-feeling part made me feel more, made me love him more. It was sort of like how a blind person could hear better than someone who could see, or a deaf person might have a really strong sense of smell. It seemed like all of my other senses were more intense to make up for the place I felt nothing. I could never make him see that what was missing was just as important as what was there. That it was one part of our makeup, the way we fitted together.

At least I wanted to believe this was all true. So it was.

And then two years later he wanted to do something permanent, change the way we fit together for the rest of our lives, and it scared me. I could not talk him out of it. He could not spend his father's money fast enough; he was in a race with himself. I could see he was sticking his head out, his chest, his neck, reaching for that finish line. I had never seen him running so fast in his life.

13.

We had taken some Advil. We had guzzled some water. We had decided we were never going to drink again. We lay there and let the water run through us. *Hydrating*, said Valka. It was soothing, and I began to calm down.

"What are you going to do with all that money anyway?" she said.

"I do not even care about it at all," I said.

"You must care a little," she said.

"Live, I guess." I had not thought much about how I would spend it. "Maybe I should send some of it back," I said. "Like half. That seems fair."

"You will do no such thing," said Valka.

A chime rang in the other room, and then there was a

knock at the door. Valka got out of bed and started toward the front room.

"Wait—" I said.

"What?" she said.

"It could be someone looking for me," I said.

"Well, if they found you, they found you," she said. "You can't stay in this room forever."

She disappeared from sight. I heard the door open, and then I heard her laugh. "Hold on," she said. She came back into view, grabbed her purse and ran back to the door. "This is for you," she said.

She came back into the bedroom carrying a bouquet of red roses. "He is so in love with me," she said. She sniffed the roses. "These are the real deal, too. I wonder where these came from, this time of year. The hybridized ones barely smell anymore. Although they are very cheap. And bright."

She lay down in bed and put the flowers between us. I fingered the baby's breath. "I knew it. I knew we had made a connection," she said.

Another person in love. I was happy for my friend but still my face turned dark.

"Oh, honey," she said. She reached out a hand toward my face. "It's just some flowers. I don't even like roses. I prefer more exotic blooms."

"It's nothing," I said. "It's good that he likes you."

"But didn't you have fun, too? With that little Prince impersonator? He definitely liked you."

I did not say that he was a she, or something in between anyway. Halfway there in some ways, all the way there in others. I knew Valka would not judge me. I was not worried about that. I just did not want her to have all my secrets. I could see that she was hungering for them. She wanted real sisterhood. It was not bad that she wanted it to be that way. But I already had a sister. Valka was my friend. My best friend. And I would tell her a lot. Not everything, though. I did not want anyone to know everything about me. That seemed scary to me.

"We just talked," I said. That was mostly the truth.

"What did you talk about?" said Valka. "Did you tell him this story?"

"Not really," I said. "He talked more than me." Also mostly true.

"Did you make out?" she said. "Did you let him get to first base?" She started laughing and I laughed, too. I smelled her roses, the tender petals brushing against my face. They did smell real.

IT WAS ONLY A FEW WEEKS AFTER Thomas and I watched the show that we were sitting in front of the brand-new Helping Hands Center in Omaha. Another parking lot, me wanting to stay in the car, and Thomas begging me to come inside with him. Thomas had an appointment with a doctor, just an initial meeting to see how much it would cost and how long it would take to fix his penis. "It's just to see what it's all about," said Thomas.

The center was a smooth, long building with windows that reflected out at the street like a pair of sunglasses my mother ordered from some commercial when I was little, the kind where you could see in front and behind you at the same time. They were sneaky. I was feeling distrustful. I set my jaw against the world. I do not know why Thomas was always trying to make me go places I did not want to go. If I had never left bed in the morning with Thomas, it would have been just fine. Let us stay just how we are, I thought, frozen in love. I had never dreamed of bigger things like some people. There was a girl we went to high school with who ended up going all the way to Rhode Island for college. She was an artist, and she had a pointy tongue that she used to stick out at people when they teased her. She was quiet her whole life and then senior year she got accepted to art school and it was like everything changed at once for her. She started wearing bright red lipstick and dying her blond hair red and if anyone messed with her she would say, "I am counting the hours until I never have to deal with you again." Sometimes she said it in a British accent. I thought she was funny.

But I was not her, thinking of something that existed beyond our flat horizon. I dreamed of the small things. Little noises, like the high-pitched squeal of the crickets calling for love, or the pregnant sizzle of bacon and eggs cooking together in a cast-iron frying pan. Or the different colors in our town, on our land, the purple and gold of

prairie flowers, and the way those colors repeat themselves again and again, the plain, healthy green of the elm
trees that shade the south side of the farmhouse, so it was
the coolest part of our home. The swollen purple belly of
our tiny town river after a storm, waves of anxious min-
nows following the flow of water. That was all, just the
little details of the world around me. There was no
plotline to my dreams, as much as I would have liked there
to be sometimes, something to shoot for in the future.
But I had no need for bigger things, no need for alteration
to my self. That was how I felt then. Couldn't I already
be whole?

VALKA MADE a little coughing noise, only there was nothing stuck in her throat.

"What?" I said.

"I don't mean to say Thomas was right about anything. And I am your friend and I will always take your
side. But."

She looked a little green, and she was biting her lower
lip. She was straight up and honest almost all the time but
sometimes telling a friend the truth was hard. I could see
she was about to tell me I was wrong.

"Don't stop now," I said.

"If the sex isn't there, it's hard for a relationship to
work. It's possible for it to work. Kids, that's one thing

that keeps people together." She said that part sadly, maybe wishing on a star for a second. "I don't think your husband went about it the right way, although I don't even know what the right way would necessarily be in that kind of situation. But if he felt incomplete, he had the right to try and fix it."

"So what are you saying?" I said.

"I'm saying maybe you weren't as whole as you think you were," she said gently.

"MOONIE, please, don't make me do this by myself," said my husband.

"But I do not want you to do it," I said. I spoke softly. I had been crying that morning, but I did not want him to know. But I could not muster up my full voice, the full version of me.

"A wife should support her husband in his decisions," he said.

"A wife should be allowed to be a part of making those decisions," I said.

"I want to be a whole man," he said. "Help me be whole." He spread his hands out in my lap, palms up, and he waited for me to put my palms flat on his, two parts making up a whole. I did it. I could not figure out how to stop it all from happening.

So I went with him, through the tall mirror doors. I

kept waiting for them to work like fun house mirrors. There would be some whacked-out version of me looking back, my belly scrunched up like a bag of trash, or my arms long like a piece of taffy. But there I was, just me, in my short skirt, and puffy vest over my tank top, and my short little legs, and my long hair, so long and straight and blond, hanging all over me, down past my shoulders, almost to my waist. I was covered in hair. And there was my husband, his hand in mine, only a little bit taller than me, dark denim shirt bound up at the cuffs, pants hanging over his same scuffed work boots he had had forever, brown hair shooting up at the ends. There were those lines in his forehead from working outside in the sun for so long. I loved them. They could look worried or hypnotized or laughing depending on what channel he had clicked on at that moment. And there was the perfect peach of his cheeks, like something ripe and juicy that showed up at the end of summer at the farmer's market over at the True Value parking lot. He never stopped talking or thinking or moving except when he was watching TV. And even then there was this energy that rippled through him, through those wrinkles in his forehead, like he was a snake charmer. He had enough energy for the both of us.

In the lobby we stopped and stood in front of a giant portrait of Rio DeCarlo, her arms waving high in the air, as if to say, "Welcome to my world!"

"She looks so pretty," said my husband. I had to admit the version of her hanging on the wall was much nicer than the version of her on that reality show, although she still had that same pencil-thin nose, the round nostrils popping out like two tiny fists.

We followed a sign toward admissions, and walked through the shined and buffed interior. I felt like I was inside the engine of a brand-new car. We passed a bunch of people in long medical coats, but all different colors, hot pinks and purples and aquas, and they all had different patches on the upper arms. The doctors—their coats said "Doc" on the sleeve—were the only ones who wore coats that were white, so white it made me think of those teeth-brightener commercials, those sticky strips that you slip on your teeth at night. (My mother got me some once and I kept gagging every time I put them in, so I gave them to my sister instead.) Everyone who worked there sped by us in their bright coats and gave us nods and smiles, occasionally a wave. A lot of people had the same smiles, I noticed. Their teeth looked like a strip of squares of the peppermint gum I liked to chew. One person after the other, their lips would go up, and there would be those same damn teeth.

The people sitting in the admissions area all looked like they could be my neighbors. They looked totally normal, is what I am trying to say. Not like they were broken, or even that they were crazy and trying to fix things that did not need to be fixed. It made me feel a little bit better about my husband, like maybe he was not alone, and it was not so strange that he wanted to do this to himself.

. . .

"WELL, OF COURSE THEY'RE NORMAL, sweetheart," said
Valka. "Just because someone wants to get a little work
done does not mean they are a complete freak."

"I did not mean you were a freak. I knew when I was
saying it you were going to think I was judging again. I am
not judging you." I swore. "I am trying to explain to you
who I was, how I was thinking. What that time was like
for me. I know more now. I am learning new things every
day. But I want you to know why. Why I was so crazy."

"Okay, okay." She shushed me. "I understand."

I thought maybe she did not, but it was the best I
could do.

I SAT DOWN while Thomas checked in with the front desk,
crossed my legs, crossed my arms, squeezed myself up into
a little ball. I would be very quiet here, I decided. I would
disappear. I felt like an intruder. Like I should not know
who these people were, and what was wrong with them.
And yet I could not help but look around me and try to
imagine how they could be fixed.

Across from me were three girls, not much older than
my sister, all reading celebrity magazines. Two of them
had nice blond hair, though I thought neither was a natural blond like myself, and were dressed like me, denim
skirt, tank top, flip-flops. The one on the right had short

curly hair that clung to her face, and big blue bulgy eyes that were lined with bright blue mascara. The other girl was just a little mouse of a thing. She had all of her parts, but it was like she was waiting for someone to inflate them all, she was so thin. I could see the bones and veins through her skin.

They were surrounding another girl who had dramatic brown hair; it was long and feathered and had beautiful golden highlights, they almost dripped off her head. She must be from the city, I thought. Her clothes were a little bit nicer than her friends' even though it was basically the same outfit. She was just a little bit more put together. The shirt had been dyed gorgeous red and orange, and there were tiny rhinestones sewn across the top of it. And she had matching red bracelets and a thin gold chain with a diamond hanging from the end around her neck, all of which glowed against her golden tan skin. She was holding a glossy magazine, and her two friends were peering over her shoulder and pointing. They chatted like birds in the trees right before sunset.

"I want hers," said the girl on the left.

"No, hers," said the girl on the right.

The girl in the middle flipped the page impatiently. "These are the ones," she said, and she pointed. "Just that little scoop up," she said. She leaned in close and peered greedily. "God, her bikini top hangs so perfectly."

"She's hot," said the girl on the left.

"So hot," said the girl on the right.

Chatter, chatter, I thought. There are some people who could talk all day and never say a thing.

My husband returned with a huge stack of papers attached to a clipboard, and I wondered if they were multiple choice or essay questions. You can never get away from schoolwork in your life. They are always going to get you. He sighed as he looked at it, and said, "It's like they want your life story." I gave him a little smirk out of the side of my mouth, and part of me hoped he saw it, and part of me hoped he did not.

Next to me was a girl, different from the girls across from us, even though she, too, had the same outfit, and also had long blond hair. Hers was parted in the middle and fell down below her shoulders, almost to her elbows. It was a pale, pale blond, as if the sun had been bleaching it for years. And her top was the color of an army tank, and it hung loosely around her. There were sprouts of dusty brown hair peeking out from her armpits. Her denim skirt had little drawings all over it in black ink. Little animals, birds mainly, and crazy swirls. I wondered what was wrong with her that could be fixed here, and I looked at her face, but she did not look any different from anyone else, personal grooming problems aside.

She pulled a notebook out from a dark green backpack that rested near her feet, and then I heard a woman say, "Must you do that here?" There was a woman sitting next to her, with her own gigantic stack of paperwork. It was her mother, I supposed. They looked enough alike—same flat nose, same smooth brown eyes with olive-shaped centers—though from the older woman's clothes I thought she might make a better match with the girl with the shiny brown hair sitting across from us. She was all strapped into place: tight pink T-shirt with little metallic stars sewn across the collar, skinny blue jeans tucked tight around her thighs, long hair brushed neatly and curled at the ends. Her nails were painted the same pink as the pink that was on her T-shirt, and then I looked down and saw matching pink cowboy boots. Head to toe, she was ready to go.

The girl turned to her and stuck her tongue out and then slowly, deliberately, pulled her hands up to her hair and pulled it back behind her ears. When she faced forward, I could see the full effect of her act: holy mama, were those big ears. They started by her mouth and went up almost near her eyebrows. The girl had pierced them at least a dozen times, with hoops of all different sizes and crazy stones with little symbols all over them. I bet her mother *hated* that. But if you are going to have big ears, might as well do it up. A minute later I realized I was still looking at her ears. I could not stop myself. I wanted to tell her that I liked them, that if she was here to fix them, she was headed on the wrong path, that she was already going the right way, that she should get more earrings. I wanted to free her. Free her ears.

Thomas flipped another page and shook his writing hand, stretched and squeezed his fingers. I put my head on his shoulder and tried to take a peek at what he was writing, but Thomas covered it up with his forearm.

"There's magazines on a table up near the front desk," he said. "All the kinds you like."

"There is not one thing about you I don't know," I said, but I got up anyway, straightened out my skirt, and walked toward the front desk. It was a strange feeling knowing I was probably the only person in the room who did not want to change something about themselves, on the outside anyway. And yet I did not feel superior in the slightest. I knew I was not perfect. I could write a long list of things about myself that could probably be fixed. But even if I fixed them all, another list would probably crop up in no time at all. And where would it end? How would I know when I was all fixed?

"WELL, THAT'S THE TRUTH," said Valka. "You could keep on fixing forever."

I PASSED A MAN with a gigantic nose—there was a hook and then a bump. His face was long and narrow and he had a sour look to him, spoiled and pinched. There was a man with gigantic folds of flesh around his chest, the rest of his body skinny and waiting for the top half to catch up. A woman with bright red hair in short spikes in sunglasses, ripples of lines waving out from around her narrow lips, which were dry and wrinkled. The aisle before the magazine rack I passed an older woman with a red scar down the side of her face, little digits of darkness around the edges. A slash mark, I thought. After that I stopped looking and kept my head down till I got to the magazine rack. I could no longer bear witness to these human frailties.

I walked back to my husband and said, "I'm going to sit in the car." My voice was husky and dark. As much as I loved him, what he was doing did not feel right to me. I just could not be a part of it. He did not look up at first; he finished the last line of what he was writing. Finally he turned up his head and nodded, then threw himself back into his confession.

In the car I stretched out in the backseat and crossed my hands together over my belly. I pretended I was a corpse. I pretended I could feel nothing inside and nothing outside and all that was left was my soul, waiting to be released somewhere. I tried to imagine flying above Omaha and looking down at the Helping Hands Center, and then over the highway back to our hometown. I would probably just head back and hover over our farm for eternity. If I died right now, I would haunt my husband for the rest of his life.

On the way home, Thomas talked, and I listened. He talked about the prick of a needle into his skin. It only hurts for a few seconds. And then you are out. I started to feel a lurch of heat in my stomach. He talked of inches, and injections, and insertions. I wrapped my right hand around the handle on the car door and pressed my left hand to my stomach. He told me about the recovery process. How many days he would sleep, how many pills he would take. How long it would take to heal. The unwrapping of a bandage like a gift under a Christmas tree. How his penis would suddenly be normal. How he would be whole. I told him to pull over, I told him I was going to be sick, I told him, "Now, now, now!" I fell out of the car and hunched over on the ground and my skirt rode up high around my thighs and a truck drove by and honked at the revelation of my flesh while I heaved onto the gravel.

"YOU CAN'T JUDGE THE MAN for wanting to fix himself," said Valka. She aimed her hand into the shape of a gun and poked her right breast. It moved only slightly. "I mean, they *are* perfect now." She smiled. She loved those breasts of hers just like they were the ones she was born with. There was probably no real difference in the end except for some plastic. "But it should have been something you wanted, too." I was not sure if she was saying that because she believed it, or if she was just trying to be supportive.

"Marriage is about togetherness," I said.

"That's right," said Valka. "Two people making decisions out of love. Not one person out of ego." She sat up in bed. "Let's think about luck. And let's think positive. We should toast to togetherness." She rolled out of bed and swaggered over to the minibar and rustled around in it until she found a half bottle of champagne. "May I?" she said.

"Sure, I got a hundred and seventy-four thousand left anyway."

"That's a long ways to go," she said, and popped the cork.

14.

One month after our first visit to the Helping Hands Center I sat in its waiting room, legs clamped together, ankles crossed, sweatshirt wrapped around me to keep me warm. Right then my husband was going under, someone was shooting him up, or sliding a gas mask over his mouth, and telling him to breathe, to trust and to breathe. I did not trust them, but I trusted him. That he knew what he was doing, that he was going to be all right when it was over. *Elective surgery*, that is what the paperwork said. It sounded like he was running for office, but really it meant he was choosing it, choosing to let them put him to sleep right then.

There had been times in the past when I wondered what he was thinking as he slept. I wished I could peek inside Thomas's head. I would write down all his dreams and keep them forever, read them when I missed him, or wanted to understand him better. Going under, underneath, that is where the truth lay.

"I ALWAYS HATED GOING UNDER," said Valka. "And then all of a sudden I liked it. Because anything was better than my life awake." She finished her glass of champagne. Mine lay untouched. I was thinking.

I REMEMBER THE ONLY TIME I went under, the beginning and end of it anyway. I was fourteen years old. I did not talk much then, not because I was sullen or shy, but because I did not have much to say. It was like my insides were not fully formed yet. It was the summer before my freshman year started, and I still rode around on a bicycle with a banana seat with thin shreds of pink glittery streamers tied to the handlebars. They blew in the wind, along with my long blond hair. It was even longer than it is now, long enough that if I stretched my body at a right angle, I could sit on it. My mother hated when I did that. She thought I looked unruly. She swore she would take me to the beauty shop before school started, and I remember it was the first time I hated her.

I was not the kind of girl to hate anyone, especially my

mother, but I was having a bad summer. I had all these extra responsibilities, for starters. My mother had gotten a new job doing ad sales for a radio station in Lincoln, and she was working long hours, longer even with the commute. She did not need to work—my father's drugstore was still doing okay then. But off she went every morning, lipstick, jacket, skirt, her hair done up nice in a little twist. Her heels would echo on the driveway in the quiet of the morning. I would wave goodbye from the front stoop and silently pray the car would not start, but it always did.

So I was stuck with taking care of Jenny, who had just turned six years old. From seven to seven, she was in my care, and I did not feel like being careful. It was not that I was wishing for danger. I just did not want the responsibility for someone else, especially not a whiny little baby, which Jenny was. She was just terrible when she was younger, or at least that was how I remembered her that summer. I had to walk her to the pool in my old red wagon, dragging her and all her toys. Otherwise she would fall and cry every five minutes, or lose a toy, or lag behind so far sometimes I would be a block away before I even knew she was gone. Sometimes we would leave the red wagon at home and I would give her a piggyback the entire way, and that was when we were closest. She sang made-up songs in my ear and I liked the feel of her hot breath on the back of my neck. Her tiny fingers tenderly clutching my neck. Then at the pool I had to watch her while she was swimming, her flopping around in her floaties. She would splash and laugh and flirt with everyone. I could not take my eyes off her for a second. She was my precious cargo, and secretly she gave me fresh hope for the future. Even then I knew my mother was so sour, and yet she had created this sweet, bubbly creature. From a pile of dirt grows beautiful wildflowers. Nobody knows where they come from; still, there they are. But if you had asked me that summer how I was doing, I would have moaned up to the heavens about how bored I was. Because all day long, all I did was watch Jenny.

And there were other things happening back at home that made life unpleasant. Dinner was always quiet now, except for the sound of Jenny clacking her silverware and chattering away about nothing in particular. My parents never joined me out back anymore to look at the stars on the summer nights. I began to forget which constellations were which without my dad reminding me as he stood behind me. I missed his hands squeezing my shoulders, the slim strands of hair near his knuckles glittering under the light of the bug zapper on the back porch. We could see so far off into the distance; we were only a quarter mile from where the farms started, where there was practically no light at all.

Instead my parents were inside snapping at each other. I could almost hear their jaws clicking from where I sat. I did not know what they were fighting about. I had an idea, but it was only that, and there was a haze around it, like the way the horizon looks after a daylong rainstorm: like the air and the earth will never dry up.

A month before school started my mother took a day off work and dragged Jenny and me around to a bunch of appointments. Jenny needed new gym shoes for school, I needed notebooks and a binder and some pens. We both had to see the dentist, one after the other. I did not want to go. I did not like the dentist.

His name was Howard Muttler and he was from Germany, and he had gigantic teeth that were so flat I was sure he filed them every night. He had a big head of blond hair, and he wore some sort of macho cologne and his shirts were always unbuttoned one button too many. He had married a local girl, Tracy Bottoms, after a whirlwind romance during her senior-year trip to Munich, followed by a long-distance courtship that had required Tracy to seek translation assistance regularly from the German teacher at the high school. Howard learned English when Tracy moved to Munich, and she had perfected her German. They lived there for a few years while he finished dental school, and then returned to our town to start his practice. Sometimes I wondered if he was really allowed to be a dentist. Were teeth the same in Germany? But there they were, with an office with his name on it two blocks down from the library. Tracy assisted him, and they would murmur to each other all day long half in German and half in English. I had heard that on Sundays they went to a special church in Lincoln, and I knew they went back to Germany for Christmas, which my mother always asked about.

"Planning another trip abroad?" she would ask, as if

"abroad" were some special place that only she and the Muttlers knew about. As if she had been abroad herself more than once in her life, which I could guarantee she had not. And their office had weird new furniture, shiny and with sharp angles. Like all the regular stuff the rest of us had was not good enough for the Muttlers. It made me nervous. I knew everyone in town from the ground up, but here he was coming from nowhere, and with an accent, no less. And who knows what had happened to Tracy while she was over there? But my mother liked Dr. Muttler a lot. I think she thought his accent made him exotic, and she had always loved foreign languages in general. I thought he sounded like what a horse would sound like if it could talk.

During my visit with Dr. Muttler, he made a few noises like he did not approve of my teeth, or maybe even me in general. A little *tut-tut* sound here, a little *tsk-tsk* sound there. I always felt like he was pressing up against me. His wife, on the other hand, seemed scared to be near me. He left me in the chair for a while and then Tracy came in and took some X-rays. She looked older than she was, like being married automatically aged you. Or maybe it was just being married to a German. Her teeth were filed down, too, and there was gray hair coming in around her face. She had a sharp little figure though. The Bottomses were always an athletic bunch. After a few minutes, Dr. Muttler came back in with my mother. He was holding the X-rays. He put them up on a lighted board and pointed to a couple of teeth. He told us I would need to have my wisdom teeth taken out. Immediately, like the next week. He asked my mother if she felt comfortable with me getting anesthetic shot into my system. *How does she do with needles?* is what he said. She would have to sign some paperwork. All these things had to happen at once. Everything was changing, that was how I felt. My mother touched Dr. Muttler's big German forearm and laughed about something. Every man in the world was suddenly funnier than my father, who was now not funny at all. It was a mess.

The morning of my next appointment with Dr. Muttler, my mother decided to cut my hair. We had been having a bad day already. "I have a million meetings I'm missing today," she said to nobody in particular as she handed Jenny a glass of orange juice at the kitchen table. My father had already left for work, his good-looking head ducked down as he kissed Jenny and me goodbye, his white pharmacist's coat loose around his body, no farewell to his wife, not even a silent wave goodbye. Looking back now, that must have been the summer he lost all the weight. He never gained it back, and ever since he had been getting thinner every year.

As soon as he was gone she started in on us, as if she was carrying on her own fight with him through us. "It's like no one cares that I have a job," she said. And we did not. We did not care how many meetings she missed, and we did not care that she wanted her own career. Jenny wanted her home to take care of her, and I wanted to have fun that summer. And now it was the last few weeks of summer, and I was going to have these teeth removed and my cheeks were going to swell up and I was not going to be able to leave the house. That meant Jenny had to stay home, too. The last moments of freedom before I started high school and Jenny started kindergarten, and our mother was worried about a meeting in a faraway office with people we had never met but assumed we would not like. Mysterious people who kept her late, away from us, and away from our father.

"I think I have a fever," I said.

"Right," said my mother.

"I'm serious." I put the back of my hand to my head. "I feel warm."

Jenny put her hand to her head, too. "I have a fever, too," she said.

"And also I feel like I'm going to hurl everywhere," I said.

My mother sat down at the kitchen table and stretched one tiny leg over another, and then put her palms together and then rubbed her index fingers together. She had always reminded me of a cricket when she did that, only no chirping.

"We will not play any games today," she said.

"I want to play a game," said Jenny. "I like games."

"I cannot help it if I am sick," I said.

My mother put her index fingers to her chin and studied me for a moment. "You still need that haircut," she said. She looked at the clock. "I think we have enough time."

"I do not want to cut my hair," I said.

"You're getting your hair cut, that much I know, Catherine. It's either now when I have the time or later when I don't. If someone were cutting my hair, I'd want them to have the time to do it right."

And then a minute later we were in the bathroom, my mother with the scissors, and me staring at myself in the mirror, a towel wrapped around my shoulders, the kitchen garbage can on the floor next to me. My mother had wet my hair and was combing through it. It felt nice. I could not remember the last time she had touched me, hugged me, kissed me. Still I was furious. Jenny was doing cartwheels and somersaults in the hallway outside the bathroom and every few seconds she would roll by the open door. My mother yelled at her to take it outside, but then she turned her gaze to my head. I tried to push my thoughts to Jenny. I wanted her to do something to distract my mother, to make her stop and leave my hair alone. *Break something*, I prayed to whoever was up there listening in the skies. And then I thought meanly: *Break a bone.*

My mother split my hair down the middle into two parts and pulled each part over a shoulder. She swiftly took her scissors and cut a huge chunk of hair off. It was at least six inches. And then, a moment too late, there was a thump down the hall, the sound of a glass crashing, and then Jenny's low whine for our mother.

My mother waved her scissors at me in the mirror. "Stay there," she said and then walked toward the sound of Jenny's wail.

I stood there, with one side shorn. Mismatched. Today

everything was going to change, I thought. Dr. Muttler had told my mother that my face would look different after the surgery. He was going to pull out some molars, too. All in all, eight teeth. I would be reset in one afternoon. I did not want to cry, but I did, softly, just a handful of tears melting down the side of my face.

When my mother returned, she quickly chopped off the other side of my hair. She let out a little laugh and said, "Really, Catherine, you act like your hair is made of gold." She was right, though. I secretly believed it was.

"IT IS REALLY PRETTY THOUGH," said Valka. She twirled her hands in the ends of my hair. She sucked in her breath, remembering her own hair, I suppose.

She pointed at my glass. "Are you going to drink that?" she said.

I RESISTED QUIETLY again that day, a few hours later. We were in the parking lot outside Dr. Muttler's office. My mother had just shut off the ignition. Jenny was strapped in the backseat, and I was in the front.

"I do not want to go in," I said. I felt like a big block of cement, and I pictured myself sinking through my seat to the bottom of the car. She would never be able to move me if I turned to stone. "It will hurt. And they are going to stick needles in me. I do not like needles. He said there were needles." I started to talk faster, and then I began to hiccup.

And for a moment, my mother turned back into my mother again. Like I had seen part of her when she was gently combing my hair that morning, and I remembered what she had been like when I was younger. It was only in the last couple of years that she was anxious and hard almost all of the time. The job was supposed to help her, make her feel like she had something of her own, but only seemed to make her more miserable in the end. But there she was, right there, sitting across from me in the car, her car keys dropped to the seat, her hands on mine, the whole world around us quiet. Like it was early morning. I felt like it was just me and my mother together.

She promised me everything would be fine, that doing this now would help me feel better in the long run. That I could eat ice cream for the next two days. That it would be over in a minute. She stroked my arm. She told me I was her little girl, and that she would take care of me. "I'll be right there," she said. "Waiting for you to wake up."

Inside I sat back quietly in Dr. Muttler's dentist's chair. My mother kissed me on my forehead. She pointed to the wall and mouthed, "Right there," and smiled her mom smile. The door closed and Dr. Muttler and Tracy moved in over me, and I could feel his thigh and smell her cool peppermint scent, and the whites of her temples looked sharp at the ends. Old lady hair.

Tracy tied a piece of rubber around my upper arm, and

tapped my forearm. A small vein surfaced. She took a needle from the tray that seemed to be floating in front of me. Dr. Muttler was organizing some of the tools that rested on it.

"This will only hurt for a second," she said, and she calmly slid it into my arm. It was true: the prick only hurt for a second, and then I felt nothing. After a few seconds she mumbled, "Nope." She pulled the needle out.

"What?" said Dr. Muttler.

She said something to him in German. He shrugged.

"Honey, we're going to have to try again," she said. "Your vein collapsed."

My heart started to beat a little faster.

"It'll be fine, I'll just find a stronger one," she said. "You're just a little thing, that's all. We need to feed you, plump up those veins." She tied the rubber a little tighter, and studied my arm, then dove in again with the needle. Again, she pulled the needle out in just a few seconds. She spoke rapidly to Dr. Muttler in German again. "*Nein,*" he said. She made another point, a little bit louder, and then he nodded.

"I'm just going to try this other arm, Catherine," she said.

"I do not like it," I said. "Where is my mom? Does she know you're doing this to me?" I was starting to freak out. I could hear the chug of the train in my head.

Tracy briskly untied the piece of rubber and moved it to my right arm. She and Dr. Muttler switched positions. She ran her finger lightly on my arm. And then—she must have seen how terrified I was—she patted my head gently.

"I'm not going to hurt you," she said.

"But you *are* hurting me," I said. I started to cry. Everyone everywhere lied.

She plunged the needle into me, there was a tick, and then a tock, and then she cursed. Dr. Muttler said, "All right, enough." He walked behind me and I heard him open a cabinet door and rustle through it. He came back and stood over me. His hands were behind his back. Maybe they were not behind his back. Maybe everything was front and center. But in the tiny little part of my brain that remembers that day, I swear his hands were behind his back, and that scared me more than anything else.

And then there was a mask dangling above my face and Dr. Muttler told me to count to ten, and Tracy was putting another needle in a vein, but this time it was on my hand, and that hurt so much, it was like being stabbed. I was crying and counting and then, thank God, at last, it was dark.

When I woke, the first thing I saw was my mother. I was lying down on an uncomfortable bed that was covered with a piece of paper, and when I moved the paper made a crunching sound. The paper felt weird against my skin, and I hated that sound. My mother was sitting on a folding chair. She was reading a magazine. Julia Roberts was on the cover. Her lips and teeth were gigantic and her hair was long, as long as she liked.

"You're a liar," I said. I said it louder. "A fucking liar."

I did not know if she could understand me, my mouth felt all stuck together. "Everyone knows." The door opened, and Tracy stuck just her head inside. "How's our patient?" she said.

"Everyone. Knows. You're. A. Fucking. Liar."

The words were just coming out and I could not stop them and I did not care. I could not even see my mother through the haze. I heard her start laughing. It was a nervous laugh. It was the first time I had ever cursed at her.

"It's the drugs," said Tracy. "She'll calm down." She walked over to me and held my hand. "You did really great," she said. My mother followed her. She held the other hand. There they were, two women, holding my hands.

"You lied," I said. I started to cry. "You said it would not hurt."

"I'm sorry," whispered my mother.

"You are a liar," I said.

"You'll be okay," said Tracy.

And then there was a shift in my brain, I steered it from one path to another, and I remembered that I loved my mother, that I should show her respect in public, that I was not the kind of girl who cursed, that I was a nice girl, I obeyed my parents, I obeyed the rules, my mother was not a liar, my parents still loved each other, a dentist was just a dentist, his wife was just his wife, and in two weeks I would start high school with a brand-new haircut.

Within two months I had grown an inch and a half

taller and my breasts were one cup size bigger. A few weeks after that I met Thomas Madison, and he made me his moon, and I took him to be my stars. I learned how to love. But somewhere in the middle of that—or was it before, I do not know anymore—I forgot how to feel.

15.

I left the house only once during the week after his surgery. Those seven days during his recovery period were
some of our finest times together. We grew closer than
ever. He was fragile and I tended to him just as I loved
to do, as I believed I was born to do, put on this planet to
take care of my man. Or at least that was how I felt at
that time.

"NOW YOU KNOW THAT you have to take care of you, too,"
said Valka. She had ordered up a full bottle of champagne
from room service, and a big breakfast, too. I picked at
some bacon, and grumbled at her. I did not need to be

reminded how wrong I had been. It just made me feel stupid.

"Oh, honey, it's not your fault. It's not your fault you love to love." She rubbed my arm. "I meant no harm."

The bacon was too salty but I ate it anyway.

HE DID NOT WANT company besides me. He did not want anyone to see him weak, and he did not want to have to lie about why he was sick. We sent the contractors home—the in-ground pool would have to wait a few more weeks—so it was just me and him sitting around. He sat on the couch in his sweatpants, the same pair every day because they were his loosest and he needed room to breathe around his bandages. Sometimes he slept on my lap and I would stroke his hair then, feel the fine flat bangs and the way it thickened into a tough curl in the back at the base of his neck, as if it were an entirely different head.

"Does it hurt?" I asked him.

"Only a little bit," he said. "Mostly it just feels like it's different."

We both read my magazines and looked at all the pictures of the celebrities. I liked to read him the bits and pieces about who was sleeping with who. There was Rio DeCarlo on a yacht with the twenty-sixth-richest man in the world. He also looked like the twenty-sixth-baldest man in the world.

"Couldn't even break the top twenty?" said Thomas. "What's the point?"

"Twenty-six is plenty rich, Thomas Madison," I said.

Finally on Sunday he let me go. He sent me into town to get carry-out from the diner. "No offense against your eggs," he said. By then it was a relief. I felt like I had to break free to visit my mother's house, just for an afternoon. It was not like he was keeping me there, but as soon as I left I let out a giggle, like I was being a bad girl. There was just something in me that needed relief.

"Say hi to your friend Timber," Thomas said as I left. He said it with a little lisp. Sometimes Thomas was such a child.

At my parents' house, there were the stirrings of something dangerous. I pulled up in the driveway and saw Jenny standing on one side of the front door, car keys in her hands, and my mother standing on the other side of it. The way their lips were moving, and their stance, even though I could not hear a thing, I knew something terrible was happening. It made me think about the way the sky looked an hour before a storm hit during tornado season every fall, the way it turned so fierce and dark in an instant. The wind always felt so invigorating, even though it was too strong for anything good to come from it. And my mother and my sister were so swollen with beauty when they were riled up. The rosy color in their cheeks, the way their eyes glittered, the thrust of their bodies upward. I sat there and watched them for a minute longer; I allowed myself the luxury of watching the disaster, and then I turned off the car and got out. Once I opened the door I could hear my sister yelling.

"You think because you're miserable everyone else around you has to be miserable," she said.

"You think maybe I might know a thing or two about life?" said my mother. "That maybe I might have gained a little knowledge in my time on this planet?"

Her mistake was saying it like it was a question instead of a fact, but my mother never knew how to handle the whirlwind that was Jenny. She thought she had it all figured out with me, but I was easy, I was simple, I wanted to be controlled.

"What I think is that you are a lonely, jealous"—Jenny was spitting now, I could see it from where I stood—"bored old lady who has nothing better to do than mess with my life. That's what I think about you and your knowledge."

She turned away from our mother and toward me. She was wearing someone's varsity jacket, I noticed (even though it was too hot for much more than a T-shirt), and short blue jean shorts that barely covered the tops of her thighs. Her legs were tan all over. Her hair was as long as mine was at her age, but she did not wear it straight, she wore it wavy. I knew she spent an hour every morning in the bathroom with the curling iron, a thoughtful look on her face as she applied heat and pressure to her head, like if she could just change the texture and shape of her hair, she could change everything else around her, too.

Our mother shoved open the front door with her elbow—wouldn't want to put down that beer can, not for a second—and shot the other hand out toward Jenny. But Jenny was too quick and skipped down the stairs away from her. Oh my Lord, I thought, we are officially town trash now, with emotional disturbances on front porches just like the rest of them. Jenny sang this weird little song while she skipped. It made me queasy, that song. Then my mother hurled her beer can at Jenny's head. She must have been pretty lit because it landed softly on the front lawn, a few feet away.

Jenny laughed at her and said, "Nice aim, old lady."

"Don't make it worse," I said.

Jenny ran behind me, leaned close to my ear and whispered, "She's crazy."

"So are you," I said back.

"No no no," she said. She wrapped her arms tight around the front of me, and I felt her belly, warm and firm, against my back. She hummed in my ear. I should have told her to just hop on like we did when we were kids. I should have just carried her away with me. I should have just watched over her right then, and never let my eyes off her again.

Our mother moved closer toward us, but then the sight of us embracing stopped her. I think she was touched. Her two daughters hugging in the driveway. We loved each other. There was love in the world, in her life. It existed.

"Leave me be," said Jenny.

"I hope you had fun," said my mother.

"I always do," said Jenny.

"Just go," said my mother, and she waved her away.

Jenny squeezed my fingers once, hard, and then released me. She backed off slowly toward her car, a little red Chevy truck my father had bought her for her sixteenth birthday. There was such hope in that car. It was a gift for the future. I gave her a glance, then stared at my mother, watched her watch Jenny get in the car. I think there were fifty more things she wanted to say, and I could see her lipstick-stained lips holding back the words in the way they bent together in a hard line against the edges of her teeth. She was not crying, but I would not have blamed her if she did. Jenny was her blood. But everyone had to leave home sometime. It was the only way to become part of the world.

At last, Jenny started the engine behind me and our mother let out a gasp of air from between her lips and the word "curfew" spit out in front of her. It was the first word to make it to the top. "You better be home by curfew," she said. "Do you hear me, Jenny?"

Jenny revved the engine and turned on the stereo, and curse words poured from the car, the rapper singing it all so Jenny did not have to. She pulled out of the driveway too quickly and the bottom of the car bumped against the curb and there was a loud crunch between the two. My mother winced when this happened.

And then Jenny was gone, off probably to a field somewhere, where she would stand against an elm tree and let some boy run his hands up and down her body like he owned her. But that girl did not know anything about love. She only knew about gratification. I walked to my mother and put my arm around her and she leaned against me a little and together we went inside to sit, as we always did, at the kitchen table. My father had made himself scarce. I never bothered asking where he was anymore. It had been months since I had seen him. He had relinquished any sort of ownership of the family.

My mother pulled two cans of beer from the refrigerator and popped the tops off them. I had always loved that sound. It was the sound of something exciting beginning. She sat down across from me and lit a slender cigarette. Behind her head were six framed prints of sketches of fruit: plums, pears, apples, oranges, bananas, and tomatoes. I remembered how we had sat around the table at dinner and argued sometimes about whether or not tomatoes belonged up there with the rest.

"I don't even think it's an 'if' or a 'when' anymore," said my mother. "I think that girl's pregnant, and she's going to hide it till it's too late and we can't do anything about it."

"How do you know?" I said.

"I've heard her puking a few times this week."

I thought of all the skinny actresses in my magazines,

flat boards in profile, and all the articles putting them on deathwatch. "Maybe she's just bulimic," I said.

There was a pause, and my mother and I both burst into laughter. We made mistakes in our family, but we were always hungry. Hungry was how you knew you were healthy. We were not that stupid.

"We've been fighting for days," she continued. "Weeks, months, I don't know." She shrugged her shoulders sadly. "It just keeps getting worse."

I felt bad for my mother, but it made me think I would not come around as much anymore. It was not that I wanted to abandon my family, but I did not think I could do any good there. Once I had moved out of the house, I had become powerless there. I would just get in the way, and I knew it would only get worse. Someone would ask me to choose sides. I was no good with conflicts. I just wanted to be happy. A girl in love, not a girl with problems. Even if they were someone else's, I still felt marked by them.

"WHY ARE YOU THAT WAY?" said Valka. "I always think other people's problems are other people's problems. Like I got enough to deal with."

"You are a liar, Valka. Look at where you are right now. With me. And my problems." I laughed at her. "And you met me in a bar in Las Vegas. A poor crazy little farm girl on the run."

Valka took a swig of champagne and tipped the bottle at me. "Well, you're not poor now, are you?"

The money. Yes, that money.

I LISTENED TO MY MOTHER TALK for a while longer, list Jenny's crimes against the family, against her. I wished I could talk about Thomas and his surgery. He had forbidden me from doing that. That was the worst part. That I could not tell her what was going on with me. And I was not even sure if she would want to know anyway.

I wished I could say, "Mom, I can't feel him. And I don't know if it's him or it's me."

And then she would hug me and say, "Hang in there, little girl."

Or she would say, "I can tell you how to fix it." That would have been the best of all.

But to say anything to her would have been like admitting some kind of failure. All I felt was shame when I thought about it.

"I thought at least this one would go to college," my mother was saying, and then she covered her mouth with her hands.

I looked at her. Maybe I already was a failure in her eyes.

She pulled a hand from her mouth and put it on my wrist and held it there. "I'm sorry, Moonie."

"It's fine. I like my life."

"I'm all over the place these days."

"You don't have to live my life, so don't you worry about it." I was yelling now. I did not know where this anger was coming from. I stood up. My whole body was tall and felt hard. My forehead was heating up.

"Moonie," said my mother. Her voice was cracking, and the cigarette trembled between her fingertips, the smoke wavering with the motion. "Don't you hate me, too."

I could imagine for a moment how sad my mother must have been. She had wanted so much more for herself, and had hoped we wanted the same. If we had been bolder and flew higher, she could have at least lived through us.

It was a weird logic that ruled her life, though she never would have admitted it: in order to be closer to her, we would make our lives different from hers. Jenny maybe had big dreams, but she let her mistakes get in the way. I was too small town though. I had small dreams. I could only see as far as the edge of the highway in one direction, and the thick forest of cornfields in the other direction. If I were a bird, I would never fly south for winter; I would ask that someone put me in a cage in a nice warm home and raise me as their own. It could be a fine life for my mother, too, if she had only accepted it as her own. She had resigned herself, sure, I saw that every time she pulled the beer can to her pretty, crumbling lips. But she had never accepted it.

.　.　.

"WHERE DID SHE WANT TO GO?" said Valka. "What did she want to do?"

"I do not know," I mumbled. "France, I guess."

"But you said she turned right around and came back." Valka offered me the bottle of champagne again. I shook my head no. "She sounds like a coward to me." Valka seemed settled with this judgment.

"Could be," I said, but I knew that was not the truth either. She got lost in the city. That would scare anyone.

I TOOK A PULL OFF my beer and when I looked up my mother was trembling. "You know I will always love you and I will never, ever leave you," I said. She smiled such a brutal smile, like it was at all these angles, pursed in the middle, down on one end, up on the other. I did not even know if you could call it a smile. It was something to see. My mother was really something.

I did hug her goodbye when I left. I had to touch her. I did not like the idea of her feeling alone, even if she had done it to herself. I pictured her sitting in her bathrobe at the kitchen table, crying into her Budweiser, hungering for the press of flesh upon hers, even just for a few seconds. I thought it was the least I could do. I wanted to tell her to be careful though, to warn her. But she was a grown woman, on her own at the same time. She should be able to take care of herself. A part of me knew though: Who was I kidding? I would be back again.

"YOU CAN'T ESCAPE your family," said Valka.

"Sure you can," I said, and then at last I took a swig of champagne.

I THOUGHT ABOUT JENNY and my mother as I drove to the diner. It was just a short ride, through the downtown and just to the other side, past the library, but I drove slow and cautious, my mind thick with worry. I waved to a few people I knew as I drove: Kira Lynn, an old classmate of mine now pregnant with her third baby, who was driving a minivan full of baby seats and drywall for her husband's construction business; Prairie, a girl who worked in the Internet café and went to school with Jenny; and white-haired Fred Folsom, the town groundskeeper, as he drove around the lawn of the library on his mower. I liked knowing everyone in town. It made me feel safe. My breathing returned to normal. My skin cooled. I was myself again.

At the diner, I sat on the stool and waited for Timber to finish his business with other customers. There were only a few down at the end of the counter, the last stragglers from the after-church crowd. Not one of the booths was full. I pictured the place when it was full; it was like it was breathing in deep then, sucking in all the life and energy and noise of the town, and then, come 3 P.M, there was a big exhale, and suddenly there was nothing left but a few gasps of air.

Timber finally came down to greet me.

"What are you doing up front today?" I said.

"I'm working the floor now," he said. "I graduated." He put his hands over his head and clasped them like a champion. His arms were so skinny. Every part of him had always been narrow. He looked like he would bend with the wind like a willow tree. "Pop said, 'I've been on my feet for thirty years, and you know what? My feet are tired.'"

"I'll bet they are," I said.

Timber nodded and sucked in his cheeks a little bit. That only made his cheekbones look higher. He had always had such a sculpted face, it just took him a while to grow into it. In school he had looked more like a skeleton, his features were so defined. The phantom of the high school. He wore a cape one year for Halloween and eyeliner and mascara and it was just spooky. But now I could see what he had become: a tall, slender, extreme-looking man.

I placed my order and Timber handed it to Papi in the back. They spoke to each other in Spanish briefly, and Timber laughed. "Loco," he said. He always had a

nice laugh. It rolled right over you, like fingers knead-
ing skin. Papi went back to his work silently. Everything
felt like it had shifted a little bit in the diner. Timber
seemed bolder, like there was a spotlight on him. I was
happy for him. He had earned this moment in his life.
And then—damn Thomas to hell!—I suddenly pictured
Timber at that glory hole at the dirty magazine store.
Timber bent down on his knees, facing the hole. No way.
I shook it off.

I had known him my entire life, practically. I could
not recall him ever being the slightest bit deviant. He
had gone out with a few girls in high school, and none
of them had a cruel word to say about him. And they
were the smartest girls from our class, too. Penelope Davis
had gone all the way to Massachusetts for college, this
very important and prestigious all-girls school there.
She was in law school now. I had run into her there at
the diner, when she was home the previous Christmas.
She wanted to help people, to fight for their rights. I
am not sure which people and what rights, but that does
not matter. The point is, he had dated quality girls, girls
of substance. That meant Timber was all right, that he
was not someone about to bend over in a dirty magazine shop, even if it was a pretty-sounding name like
"glory hole."

Timber leaned forward on his elbows in front of me at
the counter.

"We didn't see you last week," he said. It was true;

Thomas had been nervous the day before the surgery, and did not want to see anyone he knew.

"Thomas has been under the weather for a bit," I said.

"I heard, I heard." He nodded slowly. "Some of the guys putting in your pool were around here for lunch the other day. Sounds like you've been doing a lot of work over there." He winked at me. "Lots of money being thrown around."

"Like it's going out of style," I said. "It never ends." I do not know what happened next, except that I started crying a little bit. I think because I felt comforted there. I had been in that diner a million times. It was a safe haven. Like a church.

Most of our neighbors actually went to church—there were at least twenty in town. There were a lot of faithful people around. Not me and my husband, though. "Church is boring," Thomas had said more than once. "All that sitting and paying attention. It feels like class to me." I agreed with him. I did like to pray by myself though. I liked to shut out all the noise and have a clear space in my head. So there was enough room for me and God, who did not want anything from me but just to listen and help me feel better. Growing up, I only ever went at Christmas and Easter, and Thomas's dad had abandoned his faith entirely to the love of his farm. No one was missing us at church.

But Timber would miss us, and we would miss him making us breakfast every Sunday morning. I counted on feeling good at the diner. And yet there I was, tiny hot tears making their way down my cheeks. I had gone from hot to cold to hot again, all in one day. I did not like the change in temperature.

Timber handed me a paper napkin from the dispenser. I wiped my eyes. Then he put both of his hands on my free hand.

"I'm sorry," I whispered. I looked to see if anyone was looking.

"No one's in here," said Timber. "They've all gone home. You're okay. Come on. You're going to be fine."

"It's just . . . change is hard," I said.

"No one ever enjoys home improvement," he said. "It's a lot of work. You got all those people in your house, there's all that noise. And it always takes longer than they say it's going to take."

"I know!" I said. I was happy to talk to someone about it all, even if we were having two different conversations.

"Pop says I'm crazy, but I'm going to redo this place. I could really do it up."

"You should," I said.

Papi rang a bell in the kitchen. Timber squeezed my hand and winked again. "Your order's up," he said.

I wiped my eyes again, and pulled a twenty-dollar bill out of my wallet. I laid it on the counter. Timber came back with our food in a plastic bag that said, "Thanks for your order" on it. It was coming out of the mouth of a smiling cartoon dog wearing a chef's hat.

"Those are new," I said. "They're cute."

"There's going to be a lot of new things around here,"

he said. "Wait and see." He leaned over the counter and kissed me on my cheek. "You hang in there. It's all going to be over soon," he said. And I knew he was right.

On the way home I watched the whir of the fields. It was late summer by then, and the corn stood tall, and the sunflowers and prairie flowers bloomed in the ditches. I opened the window and stuck my hand outside. I thought about how those fields got quieter than an ache late at night, except for the cicadas. They made a nasty noise that sounded mean-spirited to me. Eventually the asphalt turned to gravel and I picked up some speed. I believed I was heading home to something good. I believed that my husband would be healed, and that I would be healed, too, even though I could not rightfully say what was wrong with me, though I guess I had an idea.

I pulled into the driveway and almost hit the neighbor's dog. I felt my heart jump when I stopped short. He was sniffing around our garbage. I yelled at him to scoot when I got out of the car and he looked up at me so mournfully I forgave him. They must not be feeding him right, I thought. What kind of people ignore their dog? I scratched his head and then he licked my ankle. He had long red hair, and it was soft. I wove my fingers in it. In the distance a car horn honked and the dog perked his ears up. He licked my ankle one more time and ran in the direction of his house.

I called out Thomas's name as I walked in the kitchen door, and he called back to me. He sounded excited. He limped to the kitchen and stood in the doorway. (He had started limping around after the surgery; I was not sure why. There was nothing wrong with his legs.) He crossed his arms across his chest and smiled. He was waiting for me to ask him something. I felt tired all of a sudden. I pulled out some plates from the cabinet and opened the carryout bag from the diner. I dumped the contents of each container onto a plate.

Finally, I broke.

"What's been going on round here since I've been gone?"

"Just watching some TV," he said. "Thinking about tomorrow. Thinking about that checkup." He was all jazzed up.

"It's about time," I mumbled. I do not know why I said that. I was not ready for it to be time yet. I picked up the plates and walked to the living room. I told Thomas to grab the forks as I passed him. He looked disappointed that I wasn't more excited.

He followed me into the living room and said, "You know what that means, right?"

I sat down on the couch and put the plates down. I picked up the remote control and flipped through the channels. I stopped on a behind-the-scenes look at the life of Rio DeCarlo. They were on the early years, when she was a teen model. Rio DeCarlo looked like an angel. Her lashes were so thick and dark and stared upward toward the sky. She was a natural, said the narrator. Headed for the top, only to burn out once she got there. Thomas sat down next to me.

"If everything checks out, I can start using it again. We can, you know, *do it*," he said.

"I know what it means," I said. "I'm just worried. What if it's not like you wanted?" I took a bite of eggs. They were cold by then.

"It's going to be perfect," he said. "It feels different already."

I put a piece of bacon in my mouth. I bit off some, but I did not chew it. I just let it sit there, savory in my mouth. The salt sank into my tongue.

"Come here," he said. He patted his lap. "Come on."

I got up and bent over him.

"But—careful," he said. He stroked near his knees. "Sit there."

I straddled him. I was very careful not to go near his crotch, but I leaned the top of me closer to him. He put his hands on my waist, and then he slid them under my shirt. He moved them up the sides of me. Then he was near my breasts, and then he was touching the undersides of them.

"This is the softest part of you," he said. His hands felt nice there. He looked so happy. "Right there," he said. I was hesitant to be happy, too, but the sight of his joy made me want to join him.

Behind me on the television set the narrator was saying something about a breakthrough performance. I turned away from my husband and looked at the screen. Little

Rio DeCarlo held a knife in front of her. "I'll use it," she said. "Don't think I won't do it."

I turned back to my husband.

"Tomorrow tomorrow tomorrow," he said, as he buried his head in my breasts.

16.

He left the house singing in the morning. He stood in the doorway of the kitchen, watched me wash the "#1 Husband" and "#1 Wife" mugs we used every morning for breakfast, and he sang to me. It was a stupid old rock song about feeling like making love. It made me laugh. I did not even think it was funny, but there was something about Thomas Madison. The way he did everything with such extreme feeling, held his hands out so high, his body swung with the sound of his voice, like one of those crazy southern preachers giving a sermon. It caused these little ripples in me, and then all of a sudden I was snorting, and then there was a noise coming from my throat, and I was laughing at him, with him, whatever. He swaggered toward me and swept me up in his arms, he spun me around. He dipped me. I laughed again.

"Moonie, you and I are going to make sweet, sweet love tonight," he said, and then he kissed me. It was a delicious kiss, full of tongue and moisture, and we sucked on each other's lips afterward. "Don't get me too excited," he said. He lifted me up. "I need the doc to check me out first, make sure I'm GTG." He backed away from me. "Good." He punched the air like a fighter. "To." He punched again with the other. "Go." Punch.

And then he left me there, all alone, and I wished he had not. I was not at ease by myself in that moment, and I felt the stir of something dark in me. It felt like those cramps I get early in the morning sometimes a few weeks before I get my period. They're called mittelschmerz, my mother told me once. There's no reason for the pain, but it's part of being a woman, she told me. No reason for it all.

I went to the living room and turned on the television set. One minute I was watching the TV, and the next I was on my knees praying. I needed the comfort. I was allowed to pray even if I did not go to church. I turned on the news, I remember that. I was taking a break from celebrities and their glamorous lives I would never have. Even if you had money, that did not mean you got to live that kind of life.

At first I heard everything the newscaster said. He was talking about one of the wars. There was one starting, another one ending. I guess it was just time for our government to win something. There was a picture of a map on the screen. I stared at the border between two countries. I thought about what divided my husband, my love, the man of my dreams, and myself. It was something so small to me, but so big to him. I could not convince him otherwise.

I was angry with him suddenly. He had left me alone for hours. I had been filled up with him for a week, and then when he left it was like someone had stuck a needle in me and drained out all the love. And all that was left behind was frustration. I guess I was addicted to that man, but he had made me that way. I tried not to be angry. I tried to love him because I knew when he returned he would want to go to bed. I could not do that angry. I could not let him in when I felt that way. I tried not to think of anything. The words coming out of the newscaster's mouth turned to one long noise. They were not separate anymore, just a jumble of sounds. I turned up the volume louder, but still I could not hear anything right. I tried to make my mind work, but the words would not form into anything. The noise sounded like a truck hurtling by me. I could almost feel the hot rush of dirty air against me. I started to shake, just my hands at first, but then there was a rumble through me. I tried so hard to focus. I let the noise wash over me. I stared at the screen. And then I was there on my knees praying, the soft thrush of carpet gliding against my knees and calves. I felt like I was sinking into a joyous sea of words. At last, they were my words. At last, I could be heard.

I prayed for my sister, Jenny, first, because I thought she needed the most help. I prayed she would not get preg-

nant, and I prayed she would learn to accept our mother
as I had. To not take it all so personal, those things my
mother said. Because it was not personal. It was all about
our mother, and nobody else. And I prayed for her to get
her act together and get the hell out of town. Even going
to school in Lincoln would be better than the life that
awaited her if she stayed put. I was living proof of that,
almost-finished outdoor pools and everything. My life was
not the kind of life she needed.

And then I prayed for my mother, for her to find some
sort of joy in her life. It seemed like everything was waiting for her, if she would just reach out and take it. She
should not be suffering at all. It was her own creation, this
torturous life. Jenny was trouble, for sure, but she did not
need to put every last ounce of herself into us, into her
children. She needed to free herself, though I did not
imagine it happening in this lifetime. Still, I prayed for
her freedom.

I prayed for my father a little bit, but not as much as
my mother and Jenny. All the time I wondered who he
was, and I still did not know. We had lost each other a
while ago, and had never found our way back. So I just
prayed for him the same as I prayed for Jenny, for him to
have the strength to deal with my mother. I would have
prayed for something else, anything else, but I did not
know what he needed to have fixed. He seemed all right,
my father, in his own little world.

I prayed for Timber, too. I do not know why I added
Timber in there. I just did. He popped into my head, he

was giving me a silly wave, where he just bent his fingers at the knuckles, like the ones he gave me when I walked into the diner. I prayed that all of the changes he wanted to make in his life would work out just as he planned. I prayed, too, that he would find a nice woman to marry him, so that he would feel complete. I wanted a life of ease for him.

For me, I just prayed that I could feel. That was all I wanted, was to feel.

I saved Thomas for last. There were so many things I wanted for him. I knew every little part of him that needed changing, not for me, but just for him. I spent so much time with him, and even when I was not with him, I was thinking about him, focusing on who he was, down to his very core. I felt like I even knew what his blood tasted like. Salt water. And that his bones would be smooth and solid in my grip. And if I could see all the tiny little atoms and molecules in him it would be like looking through a kaleidoscope at the sky on a cloudy day. I knew how he hated the hair that came out of his ears, and I knew that he wished he talked quieter sometimes. I knew, even if he did not admit it, that he missed his dad, and he wished he had been there with him, that there had been some peace in the end. He needed his heart to be soothed. I knew he wished he were taller. I knew he wished he were smarter. I knew sometimes he felt alone even if I was sitting right next to him. I sent a wave of prayers, I wanted to wash over him with my thoughts. Release him. Freedom for him. Freedom for everyone.

My last words for him felt ridiculous in my head. I was embarrassed even thinking them, but then I thought: this is coming from a pure place.

Dear God, I said. *Please let his body be what he wants it to be.*

I felt incredibly peaceful during all this praying. Like there was all this crazy noise around me and in the middle of it I had clear and focused thoughts. I was like a big line of lightning in the middle of a storm. I could strike, I could make something happen. I was channeling something in me. It was some kind of power.

VALKA TOOK A DEEP BREATH. "Would you pray for me sometime?" she said.

"I already have," I said.

THAT IS HOW MY HUSBAND found me, on the ground, praying in the living room, with the television set blaring behind me. He had a smile on his face when he walked in the room, but when I turned to look at him, I watched it drop away. He held a bouquet of roses in his hand. Bright red with baby's breath. I always liked baby's breath. It reminded me of corsages and school dances. Everyone ignores it because it's filler but I like what it's called. And I love the delicate crumbliness of it.

He squeezed the bottom of the bouquet. The paper rustled. He put the bouquet on the couch, and there was an even louder rustle. Between that and the newscaster's voice it was more than I could bear. I covered my ears.

"Moonie, what're you doing?" Thomas grabbed the remote control. He put the television on mute. "Have you lost your mind, girl?"

"I was . . ." I felt dumb even saying it. I sat back, and my ass rested on the soles of my feet. "I was praying, I guess. I don't know." I smiled at him extra pretty. It was phony and I knew it but I just wanted him to love me and forget the rest. "I was just worried about you. Going to the doctor."

He sat down on the edge of the couch next to me.

"Ain't nothing to worry about." He put a hand on my head and patted it and then slid it down to my cheek. And then he looked at me so tenderly it was like my heart would break in two, I could really feel that, that there was the possibility that something could *shatter* inside me. Everything was so swelled up on the insides. All my parts were fighting for room, fighting for air.

"I'm one hundred percent okay," he said. "And I think it might be time to test it all out."

17.

I had decorated the bedroom myself, without any help from Thomas. Most stuff in the house, Thomas wanted to have some say, not just because he was paying for it, and not just because he was trying to find ways to fill his time, but because he was interested in home decorating. We watched a lot of those shows, all the time, all kinds of home decorating. There were the shows that had people decorating their houses for less than five hundred bucks, and the shows where they switched homes with their friends, the disaster zone homes, and the millionaire homes. We liked the poor people shows the best because they always cried at the end. A lot of people were out there fixing up their homes. Trying to make their lives just a little bit better. Thomas totally got that, and so did I.

But I said please let this room be mine. Let me do for
you as a wife should do for a husband. I realize now that
these are meaningless words. That I made up what was
supposed to be right. I cobbled together this image of marriage from scraps of memories and TV shows and movies.
God knows neither of our parents had a marriage we
wanted to model ourselves after. It was all made up, our
marriage. Thomas did it, too. We were trying to be normal, but we did not realize there was no right way or
wrong way.

Still, I said: let me give you something special. When
it came down to it though, I made it all white. All white
with lots of patterns and textures, the curtains had layers
of white stripes and there were white flowers embroidered
into the comforter. White fluffy pillows, white carpeting,
glossy pretty white walls. I wanted to feel really clean in
my bedroom. I did not want any of that outside world, that
dirty world, coming into our marital bed. None of that
fake stuff Thomas liked to watch on late-night cable, and
no memories of that day at the dirty magazine shop. It
should just be our sanctuary.

I watched him take his clothes off. His nice dress shirt
he had worn to the doctor's office, with the pretty blue
stripes and the crisp collar, the one I had bought for him
in Lincoln, for all those meetings he had after his dad
died. Underneath there was a thick patch of hair in the
middle of his chest, and it turned me on, the way the hair
spread out like ivy on the side of a building, down his
stomach and around his nipples. He unbuckled his belt,

and there was the sound of metal hitting metal, and it rang out high and clear like a bell.

"I love you," I said. I was so nervous.

"I love you, too," he said. He slipped the pants down over his legs, never taking his eyes away from me the whole while, like if he did I might disappear. He looked serious. His legs were so skinny. I wanted to feel him more than ever in that moment. I spread my legs apart and bent my knees a bit. I tried to relax myself, from my belly on down. Let it flow.

But even as I did that, there was another part of me fighting, squeezing me close inside. A whisper in my ear. Just hold on tight. It will be over soon.

He pulled down his shorts at last, but he was on me in a flash, so I could not see it. I did not know if it had worked or not. There was the usual small, hard feeling against my leg, and then Thomas started kissing me and touching me all over, only breasts and stomach and hips and legs, fast and noisy, with crazy kisses that made smacking sounds.

His lips and his tongue felt nice against my skin. I liked the way he was rushing. I started to get into it. I made a few noises. I did not know where they came from, but there they were.

His thighs were on mine, and he was moving, and he was whispering in my ear, something, my name, his love, words mashed together. Everything was clenched inside me. Moonie, he said, over and over again. And then I became numb.

I held my breath. I held it in, so close inside. I wanted to feel. I prayed to feel.

But there was nothing there. I tried to reach deep and connect with him. But there was just a big gaping hole where a feeling should have been.

Is it possible to physically feel absence? Can you miss a sensation you have never known? It was not just the pressure of him in my body, of course. It was the connection, and it was his joy, or what would have been his joy. More than ever I knew I could not feel. I wondered for a moment if I were dead, or if something had died in me the minute Thomas and I had met. But I knew every part of my body was alive, except for this one part. I had been swollen with his life since I was fifteen years old. I was alive and young and I was healthy and yet I could not feel him. It was broken. We were broken.

I held his arms and he grunted in my ear. I knew he was moving inside me then. He had been for a few minutes. I tried to moan, and the noises would not come out of me, at least not any noise I recognized. He looked me dead in the eye, a look of love, and I turned away. I looked all over the room, anywhere but at him. My eyes felt crazy; it looked like someone was flashing the light switch off and on in the room. Dark, light, slow-motion, super-speed. I thrashed my head to the side, back and forth. I was in charge of what I saw. I could tell my eyes what to do, my neck what to do, my head what to do. Every part of my body except that one part. I kept thrashing. I would not let him concentrate on me. I would not let him see what was really happening.

He thought I was really turned on. He said my name over and over. I looked at the curtains, my beautiful curtains. The stripes were raised. They were not just white. There was a difference. The neighbor's dog was barking. They let him loose again, I thought. Why don't they care about that dog like I do? And it was not even mine to love. I started to cry. I could not stop. My cheeks were getting wet. Finally Thomas came. He laid his face next to mine. He felt the wetness, I knew he did. He sighed.

"It's bigger now," he said.

"I know it is," I said.

He put his hand on my cheek. He brushed away a tear with a finger, then held it up to the light and looked at it. Evidence against me. Evidence I could not feel a god-damn thing.

"Why can't you feel it, then?"

"I do not know, Thomas."

He put his hand back down on my face and slowly slid it down around my neck.

"It drives me crazy," he said.

"I know. It drives me crazy, too," I said.

"I thought you said you didn't care," he said. He was trying to catch me. His hand tensed around my neck. I was stuck now. Outside a car sped by, and the sound of the thick motor choked the air.

"No, I just meant that you being sad, it drives me crazy

to see you that way." I was saying the words, but they were coming out all mangled. The pressure of his hand on my throat was starting to hurt bad. I was even tighter inside.

"Maybe you want me to be crazy," he said. Now both hands were around my neck. My eyes were popping, I could feel them reaching out of my head toward him. I could feel *everything* in that moment. Everything except for his penis, now shrunken down. My eyes were wide open but I could not see.

"How can you not feel me, Moonie?" He was yelling at me, but it sounded quiet, too.

"I do not know," I said. "I just can't." I choked out the words.

"Four and a half inches," he said. "That's what he told me." Thomas started to cry. He loosened his grip. I gasped for air for a minute and then I pushed him off me. I rolled off the bed and onto the floor. I pulled away into the corner of the room. My eyes still felt like they were coming out of my head, like they would never settle back into place. I closed my lids and prayed for everything to go back to normal. My eyes still hurt.

"Just sit there, that's right, like you always do," said Thomas. I opened my eyes. He crawled across the bed toward me and then stayed at the end and stared at me. "It's either you or it's me," he said.

I shook my head, I raised my hands. I did not want it to be me, even if it was. "It is not me."

He reached out and slapped my face. "It is you."

I put one hand to my cheek. I ran my tongue against the inside of it. I did not taste blood.

"It is not me," I said.

He slapped my other cheek, harder.

That was it. That was enough. There are things a wife does for her husband, and there are things a husband does for his wife, and this was not one of them, on either end. Outside the neighbor's dog barked as if he were in pain.

I stood. I walked to the closet. I pulled out a sun-dress and slipped it on over my head. As it fell down my body, Thomas grabbed the back of my head with his hand and pulled. It hurt. I tried to stay calm but inside everything that had been tight suddenly gave way, as if I were a balloon full of water and he had popped me with a needle. But it was not a joyful release. I felt it, I felt it all open up and flood me. Whatever control I had of myself was gone.

I reached behind me and grabbed at his crotch and squeezed. His flesh felt funny in my palm. In the past I had always touched it so tenderly, and it was something special, that it was so delicate. Now it became his weak spot. Finally he let go of my hair. I elbowed him in the gut and he bent over. Then I shoved him. He was easy to take, my husband. He had never been in a fight in his life.

I ran into the living room and grabbed my car keys. Thomas came out after me and bent me over the couch and tried to hold me there. I squirmed against him. I pre-tended I was a slippery snake, I could feel myself turning,

turning, and his hands were useless, they could not hold me. Then I reached out and grabbed the remote control. I turned and started whacking him on the head with it. He looked so surprised that I was doing it, I almost stopped—I loved him, didn't I? Where had the love gone?—but then I kept going. He put his hands up and backed off against the wall.

"Enough, Moonie!" he said.

I threw the remote control across the room at his head and he ducked but it still bounced off him. I left the house, and he yelled things after me—nasty things—but I could not hear him. I did not care anyway. What he had to say.

I got in the truck and I drove. First I drove around the fields for a while. They were beautiful. Stalks reaching toward the sky, dry to the touch yet full of wetness and life. Every year, the farmers were so full of hope. I had known that hope, even if I did not understand it.

I could turn around, I thought. But I thought about the hitting, the way it was so easy for us to slip into hate. Even if we worked our way out of that hate, now we knew how to get there, where to go. We thought love was easy, but it turned out to be hard. But maybe that was the way it worked sometimes. Maybe we were just normal. That was all Thomas had ever wanted, to be normal.

Next I headed toward the house I had grown up in. The streets were empty. Everything felt empty, this whole town was empty. I wished I were full. I wished I knew how to be that way. I was crying. I heard a gurgle in my throat. I did not know where it had come from. Where would I go? Who would have me? My mother would have me, but it would be hard there. There would be so much *noise*. There would be battles, the never-ending war of mothers and daughters.

I skipped the turnoff and headed toward the diner. I was gasping. The tears on my face were so hot and salty I wondered for a moment if I were bleeding instead. I cannot describe what I was feeling as anything other than tragic. He was the man I loved for so long, and suddenly he was something else. I did not think of my love as a light switch, but there it was, right in front of me. Up or down. Up to me.

18.

And just like that, things between me and Thomas had changed forever. I moved back in the apartment above the diner. Timber's dad let me move in quietly. No one in town knew I was there at first, except for my family and Thomas. I did not go anywhere much at all. Sometimes I sat downstairs at the diner and listened to the farmers talk about harvest. I tried not to stay too long. I wanted to go back upstairs and think. I got angrier every day. I thought about leaving town, but where would I go? And it was not in me anyway. To leave.

"WELL, IT'S IN YOU NOW, isn't it, sister," said Valka.

"I guess," I said. "I just did not know what else to do."

"You better start owning it," she said. "Real quick."

.   .   .

THINGS STARTED TO GET worse for Jenny at home. My
mom put down her beer can and cigarette long enough to
slap her a few times. Once she pulled Jenny's hair and
Jenny shoved her off. I felt sorry for her, but I was too
numb myself to help, I guess. I knew she was acting up.
Jenny had four different varsity jackets hanging in her
closet. Boys fell for her right and left, even if she was the
town slut.

I was the opposite. I had had all those dreamy ideas
about what it was like to love someone and be their wife.
Those ideas were impossible, a fantasy life that began
and ended with that toy couple on the top of my wedding
cake. Jenny had no room for fantasy in her life. She was
all about the present. Instant satisfaction. The immedi-
ate touch.

But that did not work for me. And neither did the loving embrace of my husband. I was a lonely woman. I made
myself lonelier. I stayed home all day watching TV. I
read my celebrity magazines. There was Rio DeCarlo
again, same shit, different day. Like I was surprised Rio
was at some film festival walking down the street in a
fur coat, clutching bags filled with expensive skin creams
and sunglasses. Like I was surprised Rio was volunteer-
ing to help save the baby seals the next week. Like I was
surprised she was single but looking. We were alike in
that way, except for the looking part. I swore I would never
love again.

I could have used my daddy around then, a man to walk in the door and tell me I was going to be just fine. It had been years since he had made things better though. Years since he had kissed a scraped knee, or pressed his hand up against a broken heart.

Memory blurs, like the sky through early morning mist. Squint and you can see *something*, a watery swipe of reality. It was real moist around the edges when it came to my dad, but I recalled it, me coming home late for the first time one Friday night right after I had met Thomas. "I hope you had fun," sneered my mother with the beer can. And there was Jenny with her sassy mouth already, even as a kid, both of us up past midnight, and my father sitting on the steps that led up to our bedrooms. He was wearing boxers and an undershirt, and there was a tear in the side of the shirt and the fabric hung down in a flap. My mother was talking about Thomas's father and mother. She did not like them. It was rumored they were second cousins, for one, which did not sit well in my mother's mind. But also there was the matter of his collections.

"I hear he keeps a bunch of dead animals in his basement," said my mother. "He's a cheap, crazy old bastard." This part was mainly true. He was an amateur taxidermist, it was just something he did for fun. There were a lot of these stuffed animals all over the rotting farmhouse. When he died, Thomas had a yard sale and invited some of his father's taxidermy buddies over to pick through what they wanted. They all had tremendous bellies and one of them drove up in an authentic WWII jeep, which Thomas had liked a lot.

"They're just like toys," I said. "Some of them are soft."

"Oh good Lord," said my mother. "Are you hearing this, Rich?"

We all looked at my dad. He had his elbows on his knees, and his face rested right up against his hands. He was staring at the floor. There was trouble all over his face. Jenny went over and sat next to him and put her head and arms in the same position.

"Daddy, he's nice," I said. "He looks after me. He loves me."

"You're too young to love," said my mother. "You don't even know what it means yet. Do you even know how much work it is? How much you have to give up? Love is about sacrifice. Do you know how much I've given—"

My dad groaned. "You're all crazy," he said.

"You're all crazy, you're all crazy, you're all crazy," sang Jenny. She giggled.

My mother stiffened. She pulled the cigarette to her mouth. Through the cloud of smoke I could see that her eyes had narrowed. She stood perfectly still. She was wearing a white nightgown and her hair was up, and she looked like she could have been a statue in a museum.

"I could make a list for you, Richard," she said. "If you like."

My father snorted.

"I'm going to go get a pen and paper. Hold on." My mom walked off toward the kitchen. Jenny followed her.

"Let's go out back," said my dad. "Let's make a run for it." We snuck out the front door and squished our way through the cool, damp grass to the back of the house. There were mosquitoes everywhere and we slapped them off us. Dad put his arm around me and we looked up at the sky. It was a clear fall night. There were a million stars, the same stars as always, and it made me feel safe for a second. I shivered under his arm and he squeezed me tighter. I could smell smoke in the air, a farmer burning trash in a field somewhere.

"Get her sick. That's just great, Rich," yelled my mother from inside the house.

"You're all right, right?" he said.

I was still stuck on thinking about Thomas. I would do anything to be with him. I knew that the love I would have with him would be far better than what my parents had. Anything was better than them.

"I'm fine," I said.

My father pointed at the sky and started to say something but the sound of my mother's voice interrupted him.

"Number one," she said. "Lack of support for career."

I could hear Jenny's tiny voice repeating her words in the background.

"Number two," said my mother. "Not enough money spent on fixing this house up."

My father released his arm from me.

"Number three. What happened to at least two vaca-
tions a year? A pharmaceutical conference in Iowa City
does not count. Does *not* count."

He dropped to his knees. He prayed to the stars. I stood
there with my mouth open, my tongue tickling the roof
of it nervously.

"What are you doing, Daddy?" I said.

"I'm praying you won't end up like your mother and
me." He sighed. "I shouldn't have said that out loud."

"It's okay," I said. "I already knew."

"No, I just meant if you say it out loud, doesn't that
mean it won't come true?"

"Number four," said my mother, and paused.

"Number four," screamed Jenny.

"The suspense is killing me," said my father. "I am
being killed."

I threw my arms around his neck, and he squeezed my
arms with his hands. Part of me wanted him to stop me.
Because I knew I was already stuck in something. But I
could not say the words.

"Do what you want," he said. "Just be safe and
careful."

Given the choice between fighting with my mom and
fighting with me, my dad picked peace with his children.
That is how Thomas and I snuck in with our love under
the radar. I do not think my dad knew then that Thomas
would be the beginning and end of love for me. He just
wanted a little hope in his life; that someone would be on

his side. Suddenly I wondered if he should have stopped me from giving myself over to Thomas so completely. He probably couldn't have. Or could he?

"OH, YOU CAN'T STOP a love like that," said Valka softly.

"No, I guess you can't," I said.

ONE NIGHT, a few weeks after I had moved out of the house I had shared with my husband, I came out on the balcony over the diner to look at the moon. It was late, and I was lonely, thinking of my husband all the way across town, past my parents' house, past the school where we met and fell in love and became like one, past the cornfields that fed and clothed us, in his home that used to be ours. I wondered what he was thinking about, if he was missing me, or if he was hating me. I wondered if he regretted anything he had done.

And then I heard a mess of noises: metal on the ground, shoes dragging, muffled words. I looked down below and there was Timber, bent over the garbage can. There was a hand over his mouth. His pants were down around his ankles. Papi was standing behind him; his pants were down, too. He was biting his lip and his eyes were closed. My heart skipped a beat. And then Papi moved his hand and Timber laughed and Papi laughed, too, and then they made little moaning noises like they were tasting something delicious.

Even though I had never seen two men together before, not even on TV, not like that anyway, it did not seem that strange to me. It actually made me jealous. I could not have been more jealous if it had been my own husband with another woman. They both could feel the one they loved. I watched the two of them together under the moonlight, moving and grunting and loving, until they were done and it was time for all of us, at last, to sleep. I do not know if they knew I was there but would it have mattered? Their love was unstoppable, too. I went back into my apartment and wept. I cried through the night. I squeezed the ends of my hair in my hands and I cried like a little girl. I could not hide from the world. I could not hide from love. But I could not embrace it either. I was brokenhearted. I was stuck. I was sick.

The next day I started taking Thomas's money from the bank.

19.

Five hundred dollars a week extra, that was all I was taking. I would withdraw it from the bank and then put it in my oven at home because I thought no one would look in the oven and it was not like I was using it anyway. Five hundred dollars, enough so that he would notice, not enough so that he would say anything about it. It was a lot of money in my hometown. My rent was not even that much. He had to know I was messing with him. What was I going to spend it on anyway?

"SHOES," said Valka.

.   .   .

PIECES OF PAPER started to stack up in the apartment. The word was out that I was there. Junk mail. Flyers about local events. Every church in town must have heard I was on my own, so I started getting invitations to singles events. The weekly sales items at the grocery store. The electricity bill. Timber came by after work some nights and brought me leftovers that I lived on for days. I stopped talking to my mom so much. She was asking too many questions about why Thomas and I had split. Nothing I told her satisfied her, because all of it was lies. Sometimes I saw my sister. I watched her belly. I waited for suspicious movement. My hair grew thicker, and dustier. In the afternoon sunlight I could see the dust hovering in the air in my apartment and I imagined it falling all around my head and clinging to what had once been my prize, my golden head of hair. I had nothing of value left.

And then it was almost winter and the harvest was over. The night air pierced, and people began to tuck into their homes. Timber convinced his dad to put up a sign on the highway advertising the diner. Thick milkshakes, crispy golden fries. And Timber had hired the new art teacher at the high school to make a logo, a 1950s-style waiter with a high forehead. *Big Daddy's Diner*, it said on the billboard. Less of the local folks came to the diner and there were more strangers and that was fine by me. These people did not know my problems. They did not care what went wrong with me and my husband. There had been so many whispers around town. If you added them all together you could hear it like one person was yelling. My mother told me Thomas was seeing a girl from a few towns over. She was almost finished with nursing school. I did not believe it. He could not love another.

I staked out a claim in a corner booth and surrounded myself with my celebrity magazines. Timber had raised the prices with the new menu, but I had an open tab with him as far as he was concerned. When he got too busy, sometimes I helped him out with his books. I ignored his hand on Papi's ass at night, after he had turned the Open/Closed sign to Closed on the front door. Once or twice they embraced in front of me. I nodded. There was a little grimace on my face that I hoped I stretched into a smile, but it was not for the reasons you were thinking. They loved each other. It was the love that broke my heart, not the way they expressed it, or whether it was wrong or right. I was jealous is all. I was jealous of anyone who turned things right. It is a tricky thing when you are in the middle of loving and hating someone at the same time. I guess I became a little crazy, me and my magazines all around me, my dusty blond hair down my back, sitting every day in the diner for the whole town to see.

My sister circled me without actually saying a thing about what had happened. I guess she thought it was enough that she was there for me, and maybe it was. She visited me at the diner after school every day, less to complain about our mother than to whisper about boys. Now that I was a single woman, a brokenhearted woman, she felt more open to talk to me about things besides our family.

"I like too many people," she told me on a Friday night, before she went out on a date with a business student from UNL she had met in the parking lot of a boot store in Lincoln. He had rough hands like all the boys around here—he had done his time on the family farm—but he had a bigger vocabulary. "And the problem is it all feels like love. How do you know?" she said. She threw her hands in the air.

"I do not know," I said.

Timber walked over to us and refilled our coffee.

"How do you know?" she said to him.

He shrugged. "You just know."

"None of us know anything," I said. The conversation was making me feel tricky and nervous. I did not want to have to answer too many questions. Everything in my life was up for questioning at that moment. There was not a single part of my actions that felt clean or innocent anymore.

"You know something," said Timber softly. He had started hugging me every night before I went upstairs.

"Yeah!" said my sister. "You know plenty of stuff!" She squeezed my hand across the table. I almost cried, then I choked it in.

I knew nothing. Thomas and I had been children when we met and we were still children. I did not know much more than how to turn on a computer and type in some numbers. I had been halted since I was fifteen years old.

Back in school I was a rotten student, but not because I was dumb. I am not dumb. I just chose to do nothing. I thought that I did not need to learn what they wanted to teach me. That I already knew everything I needed to know. What good would knowledge do me? There was me and Thomas together forever and he would take care of me.

He promised me exactly that after we decided we were in love. There had been a few weeks my freshman year— before we met—when I still believed I needed to learn, or at least that I should pay attention in class. What classes did I like then? It was hard to remember. I think I had wanted to be a veterinarian. That was what all the other girls I knew would have said, too.

We were standing downtown, in the ragged, dusty square of land next to the library where some of the kids went to hang out after school. He had me in the corner, leaned up against the library wall, and we were kissing so slowly over and over. We loved to kiss for hours then. He would not touch me, though of course I felt like his hands were all over me. The clock struck six, and what kids were left started to break up and head home for dinner, and I pulled back from Thomas.

"My mom will yell," I said. "And I have to do homework. There's a big test tomorrow. Pre-algebra."

"Stay with me," he whined. He held my hand tight, and I could feel my flesh bend under him.

"I'll get in trouble," I said.

"You will never get in trouble as long as you're with

me," he said. "You will always be taken care of. You are not even my girlfriend anymore. It's like you are my wife."

There I was, fifteen years old and already practically married. His love engorged me. It was so comforting, and not scary at all. When you are married you have someone to lean on. And I leaned on him every time I failed a test. I leaned on him to write papers for me or to get me answers to exams from his buddies. I leaned, and he loved it. I graduated knowing nothing more than how to be one half of a whole.

I put my head down in the diner, and Jenny stroked my hair for a while. She told me I was going to be fine. That a man was not worth it. That she would always be there for me. And then finally she whispered, "You really need to take a shower."

On Christmas Eve I drove by my old house. The dog next door had a limp now. It barked at my car as I drove by and I slid down in my seat. Thomas's truck was in the driveway, and there was a red Toyota Tercel next to it. I did not recognize the car. It could not be another woman. It could not be that already. The light was on in the living room and the bedroom, and the rest of the house was dark. I imagined the TV screen flickering as Thomas flipped channels. The cornfields behind the house were flat, they were nothing now. There was snow everywhere, and it disappeared Nebraska.

I cried when I got home, and then I slept long into Christmas Day. I woke up sometimes and saw light and tiny particles of dirt twinkling and drifting through my apartment and they were gorgeous and then I could not breathe and I would go back to sleep. It was a solid day of me and sleep and everything falling all around me, the layers of dust and dirt and air and misery weighing me down.

I did not get out of bed until my sister came the next afternoon, and she would not leave until I answered the door. She wanted to show me her new cell phone. She had made videos of all her friends and boyfriends and I stood in the doorway and let her flip through them all. They had their own language, she and her friends all seemed smarter than me. She would graduate from high school next year. No one knew what would happen to her, but I still thought she was already so far ahead of me. I had never felt behind before. This was the first time in my life I even understood what falling behind even meant.

I went back to bed. Early the next morning, there was another knock at the door. There was Timber, Papi standing silently behind him, holding a bag of food and a stack of magazines that people had left behind at the restaurant. "Something to keep you company," said Timber as Papi handed them to me. We hadn't talked much, Papi and me, but we both were warm to each other. He sat next to me on the bed and put his hand on my head. "Do I have a fever? Am I hot?" I said. He snapped his hand back and made a face like he was getting burned, and he smiled at me. "I think you will be fine," he said. He left me a take-out tin of eggs scrambled with green pepper and cheddar cheese, wheat toast, and a few slices of banana and orange. Everything was warm, even the fruit. "I will bring you coffee later," he said.

I looked up but did not say anything. I could hear him, but nothing was getting through the haze around me. It felt like the whole world was bright headlights and there was this early morning fog in my apartment and I wasn't going to see anything until it was too late, the car would be right in front of my face.

"Should I call a doctor?" said Timber.

Somehow words came out of me. "I am going to be fine," I said. I watched as the words pushed their way through the fog. They were colored fluorescent pink.

"You have to get out of this apartment," he said. "It's making you sicker."

"I have to sleep now," I said.

"Promise me you will come down tomorrow," he said. "First thing."

"I promise," I said.

I slept another day. I was growing to love my bed. Everything was much easier under the covers.

And then my mother showed up, dressed to the nines. She cut a nice figure, my mother. I loved it when she wore her hair up like that, all neat and pinned. She looked French, or something. I had forgotten what she looked like out in the world; I only knew what she looked like at home, miserable and messy. At home we are all always different. She pushed past me when I answered the door. I guess she wanted to see who I was now. She kicked a foot through the papers on my floor. The dust hovered heavy in the air. My mother sneezed. There were garbage bags of old food cartons in the corner. I had meant to take them down but I had not found the time. I had been very busy. I wanted to tell her this: *I have been very busy.* But how could I explain what I had been doing?

"Usually it is cleaner," I said. What could I offer up to her? "What with the holidays and all."

"Catherine," she said. I waited for her to yell at me to clean up my room, but she did not yell. She opened her arms to me. "Come here," she said. She wrapped herself around me but I could not feel it. Something inside me tossed and turned. A bad night's sleep jammed up in my body. "I'm worried," she said. I listened to the sound of her voice. I listened for the truth. The warmth in her voice was not working on me. I had passed the point of believing her. It was a scam. She knew I knew. "You're flipping out in front of the entire town. You don't know how many calls I've gotten. Everyone knows something's wrong." She grabbed a fistful of my hair and sniffed it. I pulled back. I could see in her eyes she wanted to cut my hair, but I liked the way it was, knotted and dusty. "People talk," she said. "That's all they have to do around here is talk. You know that." I pulled back. I stood against the wall and slid to the ground. I pushed some papers away from underneath me.

"How many crosses must one mother bear in her life?" she snapped suddenly. "Why do I need *two* crazy daughters?"

I looked at her feet. She was wearing high heels. Snow was melting around the edge of one heel. She walked over to me and slid down on the floor next to me, slapping her purse between us.

"Did I tell you that your father and I are going to see chamber music now in Lincoln? Once a month, we're subscribers. It was a Christmas present. The series starts today. Festive songs of the season."

"Dad's here?"

"He's downstairs getting coffee."

I pictured him looking down into the coffee, searching for a secret escape route.

"He's trying, is the point. We're trying."

She opened her purse and pulled a flask out of it and unscrewed the top. Well, *that's* new, I thought.

"To keep me warm," she said. She took a swig. "It's cold out there." And then it only took a second before the liquor hit her gut and she turned a little mean. "He's not as smart as he thinks he is though. Not even half as smart. I'm way smarter than him."

"Of course you are," I said. I stared out into the clutter of the apartment.

She put her hand on mine and tried to make me meet her eyes, but I wouldn't. We both stared out across the apartment.

"There's a lot of paper in here," she said.

"I've been very busy," I said.

"Whether or not I'm smarter than your father—and I am—is not the point. I'm trying to ask you something. Did you do everything you could to save your marriage?"

I sobbed. I did not know if she meant to be cruel, but it was the worst question she could have asked. "I loved him as true as I could, Mommy. I tried to support him in everything. But there are some things you can't fix."

"Then let it go. That's it. It's time to move on."

I said nothing but I was thinking: I am not done yet. I would know when I was done. There was going to be something solid and fixed inside me. That was how love had felt for so long. And when the love was destroyed, it was like all these little pieces went in crazy directions in search of somewhere to land. I was waiting for everything to re-form into something new. But for now it was in the money, the stacks of money inside the oven.

My mother touched my cheek and turned my face toward hers. If she meant it to be gentle it did not feel that way.

"Thomas has moved on, Moonie."

"Good for him," I said. I did not believe her. I was weak and the words felt all mumbly in my mouth.

"I understand what it's like to lose it," she said. "I won't lie and say it hasn't happened to me before or it won't happen to me again. Your sister could push me over the deep edge at any minute." She took another drink from the flask, this one longer, and I could hear her gulp a few times loudly, like a clogged-up drain finally letting the water through the muck. "But you have to keep it to-gether, at least out in public. Keep the craziness behind closed doors, where it belongs." She leaned in close and whispered, "Keep everything inside. Where it belongs. Just hold it in tight. If you hold it in long enough, you won't feel a thing."

I clutched at her and she clutched back at me.

"Is there anything I can do to fix you? I would do it. I would," she said.

But you're the one who broke me, I thought.

"WHAT DO YOU MEAN?" said Valka.

"I don't know," I said. But it was a lie. I knew exactly what I meant.

AFTER MY MOTHER LEFT I pulled out the stack of magazines Timber and Papi had dropped off for me. There was Rio DeCarlo, front row at a fashion show, her legs spread open a little too wide, a little pink x across her crotch. Another magazine, a four-page spread of her house in Malibu. The next week there was a movie opening, and she was on the arm of a man, younger, a kid, I thought. He could not have been but a few years older than my sister. That picture was in the Fashion Don'ts section. She was the pick of the week. Her eyes were wide and messy and her dress was cut out in too many areas and there were her arms, headed to the sky. I thought of my dusty clumps of hair, my eyebrows unplucked and busy. I had not changed clothes in a few days. I was certain I smelled sour. I looked through another magazine. No Rio. She was missing from the next one, too, and the one after that. Three weeks without Rio. Something was wrong, I knew it. Sure enough, the next week, there was a one-on-one interview with Rio about her time in rehab. Her heart had been broken. She had an addiction to painkillers. And liquor. And she had been afraid to ask for help.

Oh Rio, I cried. *I get it.* I raised my hands up to the sky. *I understand.*

I could not be alone any longer. I went to the diner and sat at my booth. I had no more magazines left. I thought I would just sit and *be*. At the other booths and at the counter people sat and chatted with each other, or quietly ate their food. They were in motion and I sat perfectly still. I wondered what that was like. Motion. Outside people walked in pairs. There was a hand on the door, and then a familiar face. Thomas. My breath caught, and then my heart went nuts, pounding me from the inside out. A hot liquid feeling curled up in my chest.

I had a moment to look at him before he noticed me. His hair was longer and curled around his ears. I used to trim it for him, and blow the leftover hair off his neck when I was done. Also he had grown a mustache. It made him look older and I liked it. I loved it. I still loved him.

Then he saw me sitting there. He pressed his lips together first, and then his cheeks puffed up on his face, and when I looked in his eyes, they were two thin slits filled with something like pity, or something like disgust. Nothing like love. It was hard to tell from where I was sitting, but it was definitely not love. I raised my hand anyway, and waved. I could not help myself. A woman walked through the door and Thomas pulled her back and whispered in her ear. They turned and left.

"WHAT DID SHE LOOK LIKE?" said Valka.

"Like a slut," I snapped.

"Really?" she said.

"No," I said guiltily. "She looked fine. She did not look any different from me."

THAT HOT LIQUID inside me was freezing up, starting at the pit of my stomach and making its way up to my chest. In one moment, I had gone from deep love to something close to death. A sharp line of pain dragged itself behind my eyes, a great divide left behind in its wake. Dry earth cracked in my head. Thomas with his hand on the door. That look in his eyes, no love left. And if he did not love me, who was I?

If the insides of me were frozen, the outside of me did not know it. I was crying, right there in the back booth of the diner. It was quiet at first and then I was suddenly gasping and sobbing. I was soaked in my tears. I did not wipe them away. One part of me froze, another part of me melted. I could not stop it if I had wanted to.

I do not know how long I sat there like that before Timber came out from behind the counter.

"Mercy," I said.

"What?" said Timber.

"Mercy." That was all that would come out of me.

He helped me get up. I had to lean on him. My legs were so weak he practically had to carry me. We stood outside. There was an icy wind, and it was starting to snow. The snow blew around in little tornadoes all over the town square. My coat was open and I had no gloves and no scarf and no hat. The air was so cold I was choking. My hair was everywhere, up in the air and in my eyes and mouth. I embraced the whirlwinds.

"You might be thinking you won't get past this," said Timber. "But you will."

That was when I went to the bank and withdrew $178,000 from our joint bank account. It seemed like a lot, and it seemed like nothing at the same time. Early the next morning I got in my car and headed to the highway. The snow was writhing all around me. I went west. The roads were not fit for driving, but I kept moving. I knew I could not go back.

"I DO NOT EVER want to go back," I told Valka.

"Oh, you're going back," she said.

"Don't you see? I cannot ever go back there ever ever ever. I have shamed myself. I am a criminal."

"You are *not* a criminal," said Valka. "That money's as much yours as it is his." She sat up in the bed. "And you have to go back."

"There is nothing left for me there," I said. "It is all ground up into shit."

"Sure there is," said Valka.

And then she said the one word that would make me turn right around and head back home.

Part Three

20.

I had never been on a plane before. My life was all about firsts now. I was learning to accept that. There I was, circling Omaha, clutching the armrest on one side, and Valka's wrist on the other. It had snowed every day since I had left my hometown, though the air was clear at the moment. The pilot told us the landing strip was iced over and we had not been cleared to land yet. That was an hour ago. They were talking about rerouting us to Iowa City. I did not mind the delay so much because I suddenly did not want to go home, but I did not want to die in a plane crash either. Either way, I could go up in flames. I pictured my head a singed mess, my blond hair dust in the air behind me.

"I'm going to be sick," I said. The air in the plane reminded me of the air in the casinos. I felt myself drying up inside.

"Eat some nuts," said Valka. She tossed a bag in my lap. She flipped a page of her magazine to the Fashion Don'ts, Rio DeCarlo front and center in a leopard-skin dress, her hands waving high toward someone far away in the distance. Maybe an imaginary friend. "The other thing that works is putting your head between your legs and counting to ten." She pointed at the picture of Rio. "See, I think that would look good on me. She's just wearing the wrong shoes. And makeup." She peered closer. "And nose."

I looked out the window. All I could see was white everywhere, all over Omaha, all over Nebraska, all over America. We could run out of gas at any minute, I thought. Maybe we should turn around.

"There's nothing down there but snow," I said.

"It's pretty," said Valka.

"It's scary," I said.

"Don't be a baby," she said. "You're just afraid to go home."

"I am not," I said.

How could I explain to her that I was still just a mess of parts of myself? She thought I was going to be brave and strong like her but I was not so sure I had it together yet. It was like I was a giant balloon and someone had stuck something sharp in me and I had just exploded everywhere. And what can you do with what is left behind? Throw it away? Put it back together? It will not work anything like it did before. Something new had to be made out of it. I just did not know what that something new was yet.

"This is your reality." She patted my hand and then scratched her fingernails along my arm. "But I know you can handle it."

The loudspeaker crackled and the pilot spoke. "Ladies and gentleman, I am happy to report that it looks like we've been cleared for landing." All around the plane people applauded, and then laughed.

This is my reality, I thought. It starts in the air, way up high. It starts right now.

AFTER LANDING WE RACED through the airport. We were in a hurry to be saviors, I guess. I had nothing but a backpack full of dirty clothes and my suitcase full of money. Valka walked faster than everyone else. That woman shocked me with her energy. How she had been through so much and yet still had so much to give. Her legs pumped as she walked, like she was a stallion racing in the morning, and her arms swung, too, one fist clenching her carry-on bag. I picked up the pace. I did not want to face my hometown but I did not want to be left behind either.

Valka gawked as we walked. Mostly there were businessmen, the ones from the big companies that had taken over downtown Omaha and turned it into something bigger and brighter than the rest of the state. She had no use for them. Businessmen she knew. But she loved the occasional farmer in the mix, those people who were really my people, and she did not hide her stares. The cowboy hats and the flannel shirts on the older men, packs of chewing tobacco in their pockets. They walked gingerly with their gray-haired wives. The bustle of their winter coats. I hoped they were returning from somewhere warm. Valka stared at the young bucks, too, in their tight jeans and flat, shiny hair.

"Yee-haw," she whispered to me, as we stood at the car rental counter.

"You're man-hungry," I said.

"No," she said. "My heart belongs to a Beatle."

Jealousy struck me. Right behind it was old Mr. Misery. They both took turns slapping me upside the head.

"My heart belongs to no one," I said.

"Your heart belongs to you," she said.

Valka rented the only BMW on the lot. It did not make much sense in the snow, but Valka said, "You have to go home in style. You show them before they show you."

And then we were on the road heading west, just like that. One day before we were sitting in our gigantic bathrobes in Las Vegas, Valka telling me that I had to return home, that my life there was not done and over and that things needed to get fixed, and that I was the only one who could fix them. Then she was on the phone with her travel agent getting us tickets to Omaha, and we were ditching my truck in long-term parking at the airport, Valka promising we would come back for it, me knowing I probably would never see it again. We rushed through security, Valka explaining away my suitcase full of cash to

the airport guard—"She was a big winner, isn't it fantas-
tic?" We hustled and laughed and landed ourselves on an
airplane headed straight for the heart of America. I held
her hand then. I held her hand more than a few times. She
said I could hold it until I did not need to anymore.

On the road she fiddled with the radio, landing on a
top-forty station. The DJ was counting down the hits.
Something with a fast beat came on, and there was a woman's voice singing through some sort of filter. She sounded
like an alien, ready to invade.

"Did you see there were seat warmers?" she said. She
pressed some buttons on the dashboard and suddenly my
behind was warm.

"That is unnatural," I said.

Valka shrugged. She did not worry too much about
things being natural or not, I had figured that much out by
now. She pulled her seat back and stretched her feet out
on the dash. Then she looked out the window and started
to twirl her fingers in her wig. She was a brunette today,
the same mod wig from New Year's Eve.

"So this is Nebraska," she said. There was snow everywhere but the roads were clear. "Doesn't look like there's
a hell of a lot going on around here."

"It's not much but it's home," I said. I do not know why
I said that. I did not need to make excuses for my home
state. I loved it there. But things had shifted since I had
left. I had seen so much already, been through three states,
and I had been wrapped up in the thick air of the casinos

for days. Just a half hour out of Omaha and already the land had flattened and the buildings were sparse. There were no levels to that part of Nebraska, it was just land and sky and space. And corn, even if you could not see it at that moment. But underneath it all was the aquifer, and it brewed energy and life. Nebraska was more than just nothing. You just had to know where to look.

"Ah, it's winter," she said. "And we didn't come to sightsee anyway."

The song ended and the announcer came on and said it was time for the entertainment news. Now this was my game. I turned up the volume.

"The Los Angeles Police Department just announced that early this morning television and film actress Rio DeCarlo was in a car accident. She struck a car carrying three teenagers and one adult. We have no information about the passengers' identities, but we do know all were hospitalized, and DeCarlo has been charged with driving under the influence. Several bottles of pills were found in the car along with an open bottle of vodka."

"Holy Jesus," I said. "Rio DeCarlo!"

Valka just shook her head. "I knew something like that would happen to her someday."

"But she never drives," I said. "She has a driver. I read it in a magazine. His name is Miguel, and he used to be a professional wrestler in Mexico. He's saving up to move his mother and two sisters across the border."

"Oh, she drives all right," said Valka.

"How do you know?" I said.

"I know things," she said.

"What do you know?" I said. I could not believe she knew a real live celebrity and she had not told me. I was rethinking our entire friendship.

"Listen, honey, everybody knows everything in Los Angeles. It's no different than your hometown where everyone knows you took all of that money out of the bank."

"But why didn't you tell me before when I mentioned her?" I said.

"I didn't want to interrupt you," she said.

"Ha-ha," I said.

"And also I didn't think it was my place to tell her stories. I mean, they aren't *my* stories." She turned down the radio. "And obviously I'm in no position to judge."

I swatted her on her arm and the car swerved. "Valka, you had better tell me right now or I swear to God I will not drive a minute further."

"Hey, that hurt," she said. She rubbed her shoulder.

"I mean it," I said.

"Okay, okay," she said. "We go to the same guy," she said. She motioned to her face. "The same doctor. He does my Botox and he did my boobs, too. He's one of the best in L.A. I mean, look at me, not a line on this face." She dropped the visor down and examined herself in the mirror. "Would you know I am thirty-eight years old? I don't think so."

"You look great," I said.

"Thank you," she said. "Anyway, I've seen Rio in the office a few times. She's no delicate tulip, that one. I know

I'm loud, too, but at the doctor's office, you try to keep it cool. It's sort of an unspoken agreement among us girls. We've got nothing to be ashamed of but we don't want to advertise that we get work done either. We all keep our heads down in our magazines in the waiting room. Everyone wears big sunglasses. It's all so dramatic! We look like a bunch of Italian movie stars from the fifties. I sort of love it."

She did not have me convinced that I would want to spend any sort of time in the waiting room of her plastic surgeon. I had already done enough time at the Helping Hands Center to know how I felt about it all.

"But not Rio DeCarlo, she sashays around that office like she owns the joint. I mean, she's a funny lady, and she's always nice enough, but she's just so over the top. She makes phone calls to her manager. She points out pictures of herself in magazines. Once I even saw her offer to give the receptionist her autograph. And she walks in without appointments all the time, which is totally against the rules. 'See if he can fit me in,' that's what she says to the receptionist. Like we all weren't sitting there waiting ourselves. But she always gets in. She must be in some sort of frequent flyer program." Valka snorted. "I mean, sometimes it's just too much. When your eyebrows are halfway up your forehead it's time to take a good look at yourself. Eventually we all have to get old. Someday I'm just going to be old, Cathy."

"And you will still be beautiful," I said.

Valka waved me off with her hand. "Please. I'll just be happy if I'm still alive. Anyway, one day I was in the office for a checkup on my boob job, and it was packed in there. It was right before Thanksgiving. *Packed.* Everyone wanted new lips for the holidays. And of course there's Rio DeCarlo swooping in the door, moaning about how she had to do a screen test, an actress of her experience and stature, wasn't it shocking, blah blah blah, and she had to have a little touch-up for the next day or she didn't know what she was going to do. So the receptionist told her to have a seat, and there was only one seat left, next to me. Cathy, she sat down, and she stank, she stank to high heaven of booze. Booze and Chanel. I have to hand it to her, it ain't easy being cheap and expensive at the same time. And of course she got to see the doctor before every-one else. Although—now that I think about it . . ." Valka scratched her jaw. "I wonder if that's why they always let her cut in line, that they just wanted to get her out of there because . . . because she was so wasted and obnoxious."

"Nobody likes a drunk," I said.

"After my appointment I went to the parking garage to leave and who should I see sitting in her car but the old French whore herself, Rio DeCarlo. Just sitting there. Not starting the car, not moving, not nothing. Just sitting in her seat, her hands holding on to that steering wheel so tight I swear her knuckles were going to tear right through her skin. Staring straight forward, with these enormous sunglasses covering half her head, and this creepy grin.

She looked like the Joker in a deck of cards. And every part of her was frozen, her lips, her cheeks, her hands, her body. She was like a creature from beyond." Valka wiggled her fingers at me and made a ghost noise, and I laughed at her. "I just got the hell out of there and ran to my car. I burned rubber getting down to the exit. And when I was paying my ticket, just when I thought I had escaped, there was Rio DeCarlo, pulling up behind me. I tell you, I never hauled ass so fast through the streets of Los Angeles as I did that day."

"So she's a terrible person," I said.

"No, she's just a drunk," she said. "Everyone has their vice."

I thought about the *click-clack* of Valka's pill bottles in her purse.

"That's why I don't tell other people's stories that aren't mine to tell," she said. "But the cat's already out of the bag with this one."

I was so depressed. I wanted to believe in Rio.

"Don't look so sad, kid," she said.

"It is just that I have always enjoyed her," I said. "I would like her to be as brave as she is in the movies." I felt my chest clutch as I said this.

"She's not bad, she's just damaged," said Valka. "Everyone's a little damaged, honey."

We drove in silence for a while, quietly counting up our own damages. Up ahead the clouds closed in again, and soon we had driven into snow. I had been hoping for an easy return to my hometown but it was just as I had left it. Snow piled up high, snow coming down from the sky, rough roads, rough driving, a freezing, lonely Nebraska winter.

"Where do we go?" said Valka. "Where do we start?"

"We start with the best burger in the state," I said. And I steered us toward the diner.

21.

We got off the expressway and pulled onto the frontage road that bordered my hometown. Everything felt different already, like it had been years since I had been there, and not just a handful of days. The houses seemed smaller than I remembered, and they appeared empty from the outside. All of the curtains were closed, the lights were out, and there were stacks of newspapers on front porches wherever I looked. And there were no cars on the road, and the streets had barely been cleared. I drove slowly, and tried not to swerve, but my heart was beating a deep, deep thrum. There had been a snowstorm, and that accounted for a lot. The townsfolk went sleepy during those times. But I could not help but think that the whole town had disappeared right along with me. No one was waiting for me to come back. Maybe I had forfeited my right to ever see these people again. All because I left town.

"Ghost town," said Valka.

"Snowstorm," I said. "They're probably all sleeping right through it. There's nothing to do but hide inside right about now."

At last a car passed us, a sheriff's car, from two towns over. I let out a big gasp of air from my lungs. I did not know I had been holding anything in. I had forgotten to breathe for a minute, I guess. It took me another minute to realize: I was scared out of my mind. I pulled the car over to rest in a snowbank.

"Sweet Jesus, I am freaking out," I said.

"Drive," said Valka.

"I do not think I can do it," I said.

"We didn't drag our asses all the way from Las Vegas so that you could lose your nerve now, right here in your hometown. Keep going. That burger sounded good and I'm hungry now. My doctor says I should eat more red meat anyway. I'm iron-deficient." She paused and looked thoughtful for a minute. "On top of everything else."

Just even the tiniest reminder of everything Valka had been through pushed me to keep going. That woman was going to be able to get me to do anything she wanted for the rest of our lives together.

I steered back onto the road and headed toward the diner. A dirty farm dog hustled over snowbanks. Down near the McDonald's, the one next to the bowling alley, the stoplight at the intersection was blinking like crazy.

No one would know whether to stop or go. If anyone was out there.

Finally we got to the diner, which was empty out front except for a big rig parked crookedly, like a snake that could not decide which way he wanted to slide next. Inside the diner was the rig's driver, and Timber, who was wiping up the counter. I could not see Papi, who was probably cleaning something in the back. I opened the door and a cluster of bells attached to the inside handle jangled. The driver looked up and gave me a glance and then took a long look at Valka. He did not break his stare even as we passed him. Timber looked up, too, and he opened his mouth and let it hang there like a dog panting for water.

"Look what the cat dragged in," he said finally. He came out from behind the counter. He reached his arms out toward me and I reached out toward him and then we were sunk in each other's arms. "I am so happy to see you're alive. And not in jail somewhere." He pulled away from me and gave me a girlish little slap on my shoulder. He had done it to me a million times but I had never noticed how silly his slaps were before. "And what the hell, Moonie? What is going on with you?"

"I'm fine," I mumbled. It was nice to see him but I did not want this kind of attention.

Valka, however, did not mind one bit. "I know, she's a regular Calamity Jane, huh? Our crazy cowgirl." Valka and Timber introduced themselves and they immediately got along. I was not surprised. Valka was the most interesting thing that had stepped foot into our town since Miss

Nebraska had cut the ribbon on the new car dealership on South Lincoln two years back. They both started talking very loudly and I slid into a booth and let them gab away. Best friends forever, like how my classmates used to sign notes they passed to each other in class. Not that I had ever had one until now, and here Timber was trying to steal her in front of my eyes. But I knew she was mine.

"Los Angeles," I heard Timber say. "I've never made it that far west before, but we are *dying* to go there on vacation. I heard there are amazing flea markets there."

Flea markets? The world felt all lopsided. Valka handed him her card.

I looked down at the booth and stared at the glittery swirls embedded in the table and I imagined myself inside one of those sparkles. That I had shrunk down to the size of nothing, a fraction of my former self, and could just disappear forever.

Valka ordered some food and Timber ran behind the counter. I could smell the meat as soon as it hit the grill, and the gentle sizzle comforted me. Valka slid into the booth with me.

"Okay, how did you not know he was gay? That man is as queer as they come."

"I don't know," I mumbled. "Nobody is ever gay around here."

Valka craned her head around the diner. "This place is so charming," she said. "I just want to take it home with me and plant it in Santa Monica and have Timber make me lunch every day for the rest of my life." Her phone rang—a ringtone of "Let It Be"—and she pulled it out of her bag. She looked at me and raised her eyebrows even higher. "It's Paul McCartney," she mouthed, and then answered the phone. "All right?" she said.

I fished my phone out of my bag and dialed Jenny again, and then my mom. No answers all around. Maybe they were sleeping off the storm, too.

"Kiss-kiss," said Valka. "And thanks again for the flowers. They stirred my soul." She shut her phone. "Well. This is really turning out to be a hell of a trip."

I was glad for Valka, that she was getting such a kick out of her life at that moment. And if we were still safe in bed in Las Vegas I could have even mustered a smile. But I was not with her on the other side anymore. I was not the Catherine of my childhood, or the Moonie of my marriage, or the Cathy on the run in Las Vegas. I was just a girl in a diner in Nebraska trying to figure out what to do next.

Timber brought over two burgers. Mine was smothered in cheddar cheese.

"You looked like you needed a little cheese," said Timber.

Valka clapped her hands together. "This is the prettiest burger I've ever seen," she said. Timber stood and watched Valka take her bite. Some of the juice from the meat dripped down her hands and Valka licked it up gingerly. "Delish," said Valka. Timber just smiled and stared at her. He was in love with her as much as I was, any fool could see that.

She took another bite and then put her burger down. "Now," she said. "We just need a plan."

"I don't even know where to start."

"What do you need a plan for?" said Timber.

"We're here on a mission," said Valka. "A secret mission."

"Tell me more," said Timber.

And then Valka said the same word to Timber that she said to me in Las Vegas to get my ass on the plane.

Jenny. It was all about Jenny, of course.

Jenny, and that tiny little life bubbling up inside her. Jenny's arm in a sling. Our mother waiting for another chance to teach her a lesson. Jenny trapped in that house forever, or out in the snow somewhere, worse or better, I could not decide. Jenny making the wrong decisions. The decisions being made for her. My little sister, lost and alone and hurt. Doing her crooked cartwheels so no one would notice what was wrong with me. Jenny with her hands on her hips, looking at me.

Where do you think you're going, missy?

"Timber, where is my sister?" I said.

Timber shook his head and sat down next to me in the booth.

"Your mom's got her over at the house. She said she took away her car keys, locked her up in her bedroom, and she's been telling everyone she's not letting her out till spring." Timber looked at me kind of funny. "We all were just kind of hoping she was kidding."

"But what about the baby?" I said.

"There's a baby?" said Timber.

"Uh," I said.

"I don't know anything about any baby. She's been telling everyone that Jenny said she was going to run away. To find you." He put his hand on mine. "Looks like you're her hero."

It was not possible I could be anyone's hero. But when I looked at Valka she was nodding, and when I looked at Timber he was nodding. I did not nod back.

In the end, we did not need much of a plan. We just got in the BMW and drove to my parents' house, Timber following us in his truck. Although we did act like we were secret agents as we were walking out the door of the diner. Valka sang the theme song to *Mission Impossible* and Timber pretended to shoot imaginary criminals and did a dive into the snow. If we had known what we were going to face when we got there, we would not have acted so carefree.

22.

No one had cleared the snow from the driveway at my childhood home. At every other house on the block the massive drifts had been pushed aside onto front lawns and sidewalks. At our house, the snow piled up above the bottom of the front porch and around Jenny's car all the way to the windows. Giant, swirling icicles hung everywhere, blocking the windows and the garage. I noticed for the first time that the right side of the roof was sagging. Had it always been that way and I had just never noticed? It was starting to get dark, and a new layer of chill crept over me.

"I have never seen snow like this in my life," said Valka, as we waded toward the front door. "It must crush the spirit."

"I don't mind it," said Timber. "You kind of buckle up

and go for the ride. And just when you think there's no chance for hope, that you'll never see another black-eyed Susan—"

"—or the cornfields," I said.

"—or an American elm," said Timber.

"—or cranes on the Platte," I said.

"Then there's spring," he said.

Valka laughed at the both of us, at our spring fancying.

"We love Nebraska," I said.

"We do," said Timber.

We reached the front door and I stood, ankle-high in the snow, and tried to unlock it. The dead bolt was locked. I did not have a key for it. It was something my mother had put in years ago, when there had been a mass murder at a Wendy's near the Walmart where my dad worked. The killer had taken his ex-girlfriend and all of her coworkers into the deep freezer and shot them all execution-style. The police found the bodies bent over gallon jugs of ketchup and mustard. The killer made it all the way to the Canadian border but was stopped by the guards there. Wrestled to the ground. Screaming holy hell. They showed him in cuffs on the TV. He was a local boy, just like the rest of us. But he had gone mad for love. My mother muttered about the crazies for a few weeks and then finally one night my father pulled out his drill and installed the dead bolt. We used it just at night. Just to keep the crazies away. Crazies like me.

"She does not want me here," I said. I pointed at the door. "She used the extra lock."

"Too bad," said Valka. "You're here." She sounded tough and masculine. She could crush someone at any moment.

We stood for a moment, balancing ourselves in the snow.

"We could throw something through a window," said Valka.

"Or climb up to the second floor," said Timber.

"Or we could just walk around the house and use the back door," I said.

They both booed me.

"You are like the least fun superhero ever," said Valka.

We trudged around back through the snow, all of us taking turns at tipping over. I eyed the right side of the roof as we passed it. It looked like the house was shedding itself, scallops of siding dripping down toward the ground. That could not have just happened this winter.

We rounded the corner, past the shivering, barren elms and the tips of the thatched wire fence that bounded what was once my mother's vegetable garden. When we were little we would help dig up potatoes with her, and then she would slice and fry them and make fresh French fries for dinner. She stopped gardening once we got older, but there was still rosemary and a handful of lonely potatoes every summer.

I heard a cough and looked up. It was my father sitting on the bench on the back porch. He had a glass in his hand filled with brown liquor and ice. He was smoking, something I had not seen him do for years. I moved faster, leaving Valka and Timber behind. As I got closer I could see he was as skinny as a stray cat begging for scraps. It was so quiet, except for the sound of us wading. He coughed again. The sky was gray. My father was surrounded by snow, which he had dug out and molded to make a sort of chair for himself, including arm rests. A bottle of whiskey and a ring of cigarette butts sat at his feet. Valka fell again and shrieked, and he looked up.

"Well, looky-here," he said. "Miss Catherine." He had never taken to calling me Moonie. I was named after his mother. "I thought you'd be in Hawaii by now. Doing the hula." He did a halfhearted sway with his hands to one side and then another. Oh, he was ripped.

"Dad, what's going on in there?" I said.

"Well," he said and leaned back, resting his arms on the snow. "Something's come over your mother."

His skin was white and the circles under his eyes hung down a few rungs.

"You know what I mean," he said.

Yes, I did.

23.

Something had been coming over my mother my entire life. We all knew it, in my family. We all knew my mother had been wounded. We all knew she was only sometimes healed, and if it was only sometimes, it was probably not at all. We never talked about it. We never told a soul. We were all in her shame with her. In it so far we could not make our way out again.

I had been keeping my secrets for so long. Other people's secrets. I took everyone's pain for my own. But when I left my husband, when I lost my mind, when I stole all the money, when I hit the road, when I saw the mountains build in the distance until I was right up next to them, so close it seemed I could have climbed right to the top, when my world unfolded before my eyes, all I had wanted to do the whole time was tell someone this one thing. I could not tell Valka. It just seemed too dangerous to give it all to her, and I needed her too much. But I could tell someone else. Someone new. And I had.

AT 5 A.M. ON NEW YEAR'S EVE, Valka and Paul McCartney were making out in the other room. I could hear the low laughter and sometimes there was a loud smack of the lips. Britney Spears had been the last one at the party, and they had finally booted her out. ("Y'all are gonna miss me when I'm gone," she screeched.)

It was dark in the bedroom except for light coming through the curtain on the French doors. Prince crawled across the bed toward me like a cat and when he got to me he let out a meow and we both laughed.

"I wanna lap you up," he said.

"Oh," I said. "I don't know." I was dizzy, and then there was that clenching-up feeling inside.

"Come on," he said. "Just let me love you for a little while." He put his face close to mine. He smelled spicy.

I blurted it out: *I have a hard time feeling.* It was so nice to say it out loud, even though I felt humiliated at the same time. I hoped it would get better as time went on. I could not go back to not saying it again. I knew that much.

"I know, baby," he said. "It's a rough world. People have a hard time letting go." He ran his hand down the side of my face, a fingertip down my neck, a full hand again on the top of my chest, and the side of my breast, and finally down to my hip. A warm trail followed his hand on the outside, but on the inside I was chilled. "You just have to relax." He moved his hand to my hip.

"I can't." I started to cry and choke a bit. *He is going to do it anyway*, that is what I was thinking.

I know now it makes no sense to think that way. But that was just what I had always believed. That thought was stuck deep inside me.

"Okay, okay, baby," said Prince. "You calm down now." Prince pulled his hand away from my stomach. Of course, I was freaking him out. Of course. I am a freak. But then he put his hand in mine, and lay down next to me.

"You want to know about not feeling?" he said. "I got that covered."

Prince started talking and told me stories from when he was still living his life as a girl in Memphis. Tough enough being mixed race, let alone feeling like she was supposed to be someone else entirely. Girls looking away in locker rooms, when she got caught staring. Boys treating her rough in the hallways and after school.

The story ended with her mother catching her making out with her lab partner and kicking her out of the house.

"It was actually a relief," Prince told me. She cut off her hair. She bound her breasts. She changed her clothes. There were a lot more lab partners out there, just waiting for a girl like her. A man like him.

When she was done talking, I said, "You win." He had

been through the wringer, just like me. Thrown out into the world by his mother. He had turned into something new though. All I had done was steal a bunch of money.

"What do I win? Do I win you?"

I took a deep breath. "Okay." I shifted and then started to unbutton my shirt.

Prince laughed. He was not being mean, but still it stung. Then he pushed my hands away gently from my shirt. "What kind of man do you think I am? I don't want to make you do anything. We can just talk. Come on, you tell me. Tell me your hard-luck story. I promise not to laugh at you or judge you or say anything to make it worse. We're just two strangers meeting for a night. You can trust me."

Our faces were so close.

"It is not my story," I said. "It is my mother's. The bedtime story she used to tell me."

"If she told it to you, it's yours, too."

I turned up toward the ceiling. I sucked in some air and held it and then burst it out when I could not stand it for a second longer.

HOW DID THAT STORY go again? The one she was always whispering in my ear before bedtime. Hovering with that wine breath. Watery eyes. Fingers that pinched. Sometimes there were stories about my father, about what a waste of time he was. In bed, in life. *And when I wake up in the morning, he is still there.* She made that sound like a bad thing, but I always knew it was good. That someone would be there in the morning. She rattled off her complaints. Her voice swerving. I knew she was just complaining, but it made me sad anyway. I could handle sad. But then there was the one story that scared me.

How did it go? It started in Omaha. A college girl heading to France, her first time away from home. She was wearing a hat she had bought at the Brandeis department store that looked like one she had seen in a magazine. A white summer hat with a wide, creamy ribbon around it. There was an early morning plane to Chicago, another to New York City, a flight to Paris, and then she would have to take a commuter train to Rennes, where she would live at the university there. More than a day of travel. Out-of-her-mind tired. Her first time on a plane, her first time anywhere. Big eyes for the world.

She had felt cool and confident when she left in the morning, but on the plane to Paris she was a mess. Her linen dress was wrinkled. Her blue eyeliner was smudged around the corners of her eyes, the matching shadow falling down her cheeks. The pins in her hair kept jamming into her head. She took her hair down. She washed her face in the bathroom. You are a mess, is what she said to herself in the mirror. *A target*, she realized later. A single woman traveling alone. Anyone could have seen it. Especially the man in the suit across the aisle, a man just short of her daddy's age, if he were still alive. He would have been happy she went to France. He would have been scared the whole time she was gone and never told her a thing but he would have been happy. Did not matter anyway. He was dead now, three years past. She was on her own now. Whether she wanted to be or not. But here was this man across the aisle. He did not want her to be alone.

What did he look like? I asked that once. When I thought it was just a bedtime story. Maybe I asked the first time she told the story. Never again. I never asked another question again.

He was muscular, but short. He had a thick jaw. He had brown hair, and he wore it a little long. He had young hair, but an old face. He had big hands. His teeth were white and huge. He wore an expensive suit. It was cut tight around him. He filled out his suit. He filled out the seat he was sitting in. He took up all the room around him he possibly could. He was an ice-cold block of a man.

He was chewing gum. He offered her a stick. She took it. He spoke to her in French.

Coming home?

I am visiting.

Oh, you looked French to me. This hat, this dress. So French.

My mother was flattered.

I am American.

He smiled painfully at my mother. Then he started speaking in English to her and she was relieved. She knew she was going to have to speak in French the entire time once she landed. This was the point of her going. But she was not totally ready. To give in to being on her own. In her head, on her own.

What did they talk about? That part I do not remember. Maybe she told me once. I remember the gum, and that she told him she was American, and that they talked for a while. He asked her questions, she answered. She asked him questions, and he told her very little. He was a scientist. A man of science. He was coming home from a conference. That was all she knew. He was more interested in her. In her being an orphan, in her being alone, in this boy she had just met at an ice cream social at school, but, no, he was not her boyfriend. Yet. He was most interested in her having to find her way to the train all by herself.

They walked off the plane together. She pulled out the letter that had been sent to her by the immersion program. It contained all the directions to the train she would take to Rennes. There was a phone number. She was dizzy. The airport was huge. It was late in the afternoon, but it could have been any time at all.

Let me see those directions. I will tell you what you need to do.

She handed him the directions.

He scanned the paper.

These directions they give you, they are all wrong.

He ripped the piece of paper into little pieces, walked to a garbage can, and threw them away. My mother watched him, horrified.

I know exactly where this is. I will show you the way.

He took her arm. She stared at him.

No, it's fine, I promise. I know where we go. We take the metro right there.

She stared back at the garbage can for a moment. And then she went with him.

He took her on the metro, all right. Around the city for hours. Off one train and on another. A loop. She had never been on a subway before. He kept her talking the entire time. She tried to pick up bits and pieces of conversation from other people but he would not let her leave his attention. Sometimes he would tell her they should just get off the train and have coffee. She shook her head.

You meet me for a coffee when you come back to Paris, yes? We go to the café. I take you to a beautiful café.

He kept touching her knee.

She felt herself crumbling. She just wanted to stop traveling.

They finally arrived at the station. He left her in the corner with her backpack. She could have run, but where would she have gone? She thought she was trapped. Trapped in a train station in France.

Oh, my poor mother.

He walked to the ticket counter. Of course, the last train had left. Of course, she must stay with him at his home. He insisted. Just one more train ride away.

Every part of her sank down, until she was flat on the ground. He picked up her bag. He grabbed her hand and pulled her up. She dragged her feet, and he put his hand on the small of her back. She took her hat off her head. Her hair smelled. It felt dirty, and heavy on her head.

I like this, he said. He wrapped his hand in the end of her hair for a second. She looked him in the eye.

Come on, it will be okay, he said. *Everything will be okay.*

They took another subway. He lived six stops away. How had he not known how to get there? He had known, of course he had known. They walked out of the station. It was night then. Late. Would he just let her go to sleep? she asked him. Could she just. Sleep.

Don't you want to take a shower first?

They walked for a while, through the suburbs of Paris. The streets were quiet and damp, like it had just rained. All the lights were out in town. The street signs were in French, but otherwise they could have been anywhere. And the houses there all looked the same as the next, just like they did in the suburbs of Omaha. She had gone all that way just to go back to where she started.

His house had three stories and was narrow. Every room was carpeted. There was no furniture in the living room except for one chair. There was a small kitchen. He opened the refrigerator door. It was empty.

There is nothing to eat, he said. *Sorry.*

She followed him up the stairs. There were two rooms on the second floor. One door was open, and there was a mattress on the floor.

I have a friend who sleeps here sometimes, he said.

On the third floor there was a bedroom with a king-sized bed, draped in satin sheets. A closet with mirrors for doors. One of the doors was open. It was full of suits. He dropped her bag on the floor. There was a bathroom attached to the room.

Let's go, he said. *Time to shower.* He took her by the arm.

I just want to sleep, she said.

First, you shower.

She walked into the bathroom. The tiles on the wall were brown. He followed her. She turned and faced him.

What if I don't want to take a shower?

He put his hand in her hair. He stroked it. He turned it around in his hand, caught it up in his fist.

You have been traveling so long. You will feel better after you shower.

I don't want to, she said.

He gathered up more of her hair in his fist, twisted it tight, and then slammed her head against the wall.

"THAT WAS ALWAYS THE PART that made me cry when I was a kid. Every time I heard it. Somebody hurting my mother. That was the worst thing in the world I could think of," I said.

I was curled up tight against Prince. His hand was in my hair, and he kept stroking it, and I liked it.

"It scared me," I said to Prince. "I have been scared forever."

"No one should tell a little kid those kinds of stories," said Prince. "It wasn't right, what your mother did. I am sorry for her pain, but you cannot lay that kind of thing on a child."

"It was our secret, I guess." I pulled up closer to Prince. I kissed him.

"You don't have to do that," he said. "We can just lie here. It's late, and you're feeling all kinds of emotions right now."

But the kissing felt necessary to me. I was desperate for Prince to touch me. I got up on my knees and pulled up my dress from the bottom, up over my thighs and hips, up over my breasts, till I stood there naked in front of him. "Well, there you go," he said. He moved one hand over me, then got up on his knees, too. He put both hands on my breasts. "They're so nice," he said. He kneaded them, then he started sucking on my neck with giant juicy kisses. They spread from my neck to my face and then my lips. There was his tongue in my mouth. He licked the inside of my mouth. Then there were kisses down my body and he had his hands on my ass and then behind my thighs. He pushed me back calmly. "Let me lay you down," he said. He ran his hands all the way up and down, then very gently down the insides of my legs. Prince rubbed his palm on the outside of my crotch, and it warmed up. And then he leaned over and blew on it and it was like a wind to a flame.

That was when I started making all kinds of noises. I must have sounded like a real loon to him. But holy moly, I was feeling good.

Then he put one finger inside me, and I clenched up. He knew it, too. I stopped making noises. I was just concentrating. He put another finger inside me and moved them back and forth slow only for a minute. "Do you like it?" he said. He looked at me. He would not let me look away. I was thinking too much, though.

So he pulled his fingers out of me, dropped down and blew on me some more, before he started licking me up and down. I asked him to keep going. Okay, I begged him. I had my hands up to my breasts and I was pinching my nipples. It took nothing, just a minute of that, and then I came, his tongue still inside me. Then he pulled back, his face damp with my wetness, and said, "That's right, baby girl." Then he pressed his palm against my crotch again and then stretched his other hand around my neck and stared at me. He waited until my breathing calmed down.

"I don't want to hurt you," he said.

"You're not," I said. "You won't."

He put a finger in me. "So wet," he said, and then he put in another, and moved back and forth. He put his hand to my face. "Can you feel me?" I shook my head. I looked down at his hand. He pulled back and then put another finger in me. I shuddered a little bit. "You're starting to feel me now, aren't you?" It was true, I was. It was like I was staring at the sky and all of a sudden a shooting star went by me. There was something new in my universe. He moved his hand back, and there was another one, another finger deep inside me. I held my breath and looked up at the ceiling. I was feeling everything at once. And then there was the last finger. I cursed. I cursed loudly. I cursed my fears. I cursed my mother. I cursed the past. And then I came into the future.

24.

I moved next to my father and knelt close. The snow soaked through my jeans.

"Where's Jenny?" I said.

"My stomach's on fire," he said. He rubbed his belly and licked his lips around the corners.

"Dad, where is Jenny?"

"She's upstairs, I think. Your mother's got her locked up there in the bedroom."

I took the drink from his hand.

"This is not you," I said.

"Are you hungry?" said Timber. "When was the last time you ate something?"

My father looked at Timber and opened his mouth and then nothing came out. Then he just started nodding.

Timber waded toward him and lifted him up. "I'll take care of you," he said to my father. "We'll set you up real good." They struggled off together in the snow toward the front of the house, Timber telling him all the things he was going to feed him. Chicken noodle soup. A big bowl of chili. Cheeseburgers.

I turned to Valka. Her eyes were bigger than ever. "I swear they were not this crazy when I left," I said. "They got stuck in the snow, I think."

I slid open the back screen door and we walked in silently. Inside the kitchen looked the same as always but maybe worse for the wear. The orange tile of the kitchen floor was beat down with a brown film. There were three ashtrays on the kitchen table, all overflowing with butts. Some were stubbed out, and some my mother must have lit and just forgotten to smoke. Beer cans everywhere. It stank to high heaven. There was a pile of broken glass in the corner. I looked around the corner to the living room. Two chairs were overturned.

"The scene of the crime," said Valka. "I'm surprised there isn't a chalk outline. Or a hooker passed out somewhere."

"Let's go get Jenny," I said. We ran upstairs. I tried the handle on the door. New locks had been installed. I did not know when that had happened.

I banged on the door. "Are you in there?"

"She locked it from the outside," said Jenny. "You need a key."

"I got this," said Valka. She shook the door handle, then peered closely at it. "We need a knife," she said. "Like a really thin knife."

I ran back down to the kitchen and rummaged through the silverware drawer. Something in the sink caught my eye and I stopped where I stood. I looked back over toward the sink slowly. Inside it was a massive pile of blond hair. Jenny's pride.

My mother walked around the corner from the living room. She was wearing a housedress and held a cigarette and a can of beer. Her lipstick was perfect. Her hair was held high, but her head hung low. I crossed my arms and looked at her.

She crossed her arms right back at me and said, "When will you girls learn?"

I pulled out a knife from the drawer. "Sit," I said.

My mother waved her hands in the air. "Fine, fine." She slumped down at the kitchen table.

I reached my hand out to her. "Give me the key."

"I swallowed it," she said.

"You're insane," I said.

"Oh, please," she said. "You and I are the exact same kind of crazy and you know it."

I pointed a finger at her. "Do not move," I said.

She flapped her hands in the air. "Where the hell would I go?" she said.

I ran back upstairs and handed the knife to Valka. She slid it between the door and the frame, jiggled it a few times, and the lock popped open.

Inside the room Jenny was sitting on her bed. Her knees were up to her chest. She had a small bowl of hair left around her head. The walls around her were bare. All her posters of hip-hop stars were gone. The fall football schedule. Every single wrist corsage she had ever been given. The calendar where she counted down the days till graduation. A collage of movie stars she admired. Everything was gone. It was just Jenny alone in her bedroom with a bad haircut and a baby in her belly.

"We're busting you out of here," said Valka.

Jenny looked at Valka.

"Where are we going?" She sounded hard.

"Away from the mean lady," said Valka. Jesus, Valka really did not get kids.

"You know, I don't even care about this baby," she said. "I could care less."

"Do not say that, Jenny," I said.

"Keep it, kill it, whatever." She curled herself up into a ball even further. "It doesn't matter to me. It's just another thing that's happened to me."

I crawled over on the bed next to her and put my arms around her. "Jenny, you are just going through some hard times right now. No one has been looking out for you. I am sorry. But I have come to get you."

"I've been in this room for two days," she said. "Mom said I needed to think about what I had done. I have been thinking. And I do not care. I did not care when I was having sex with those men. I couldn't hardly feel it even. I don't feel anything. That's why I do it so much. To see if I can ever feel." She looked at me. "I can't feel, Moonie. I'm a freak. What is wrong with me?"

I felt a horrible something inside me. It was hotter than hell. It was not just me that was this way. I wanted to run outside and throw myself into a snowbank. It would be the only way to cool down. I wanted the Nebraska winter to take me whole.

HOW DID THAT STORY GO AGAIN? The one she told me a hundred times. Leaning in so close, her whisper sounded like thunder in my ear.

In the bathroom, she took off her clothes. He looked at her and grunted. She got in the shower. He turned on the water. He took off his clothes and got in the shower. He took some soap from a dish and began to wash her.

See, it is not so bad to get clean.

She tried to let it feel good but it did not. She started to cry.

Don't cry, he said. He was annoyed.

I want to go home, she said.

He looked at her, bored. He turned her around, then bent her over in half. Easily, like she was a rag doll. She squeezed her legs together.

Stop that, he said. He forced her legs open. He rubbed the soap all over her. He forced himself in, and she squeezed her insides tight.

That ever happens to you, you just squeeze tight, she

told me. Pretend you're frozen shut in there. Pretend it's broken. Pretend you are somewhere else. Pretend you are anywhere else but right there. Pretend you are not you. Pretend what you need to pretend to not feel a goddamn thing.

And that was when he shoved himself in her ass. Because he wanted to make sure she felt it.

OH, JENNY, I THOUGHT. You, too.

She was ranting.

"And if I can't feel, then I don't care, and if I don't care, then I'll do whatever Mom wants with this baby."

"I don't think that's right," said Valka softly.

"This is my friend Valka," I said to Jenny.

"You shouldn't talk that way," said Valka.

"I'll talk however I want," said Jenny. "You don't know what I'm going through. You don't know me. You don't know a goddamn thing."

"I know I don't know you," said Valka. "And I am not going to tell you that you are right or wrong about who you sleep with or how many people. It takes all kinds in this world, and I'm not one to talk anyway. And I don't even care if you decide to keep that baby or have an abortion or give it up for adoption or whatever else you could choose to do. But you should have more respect for your insides. The fact that you can conceive, that your body works in that way. You should not be careless about your power. There are people who would kill to have that power. You should appreciate it. It's your body. You do what you want with it. But you respect it."

Jenny burst into tears. And then Valka burst into tears. And then what was I to do but cry, too? We all sat there on the bed and had ourselves a good cry. I cried for my mother more than anything, and for how my family would never be the same again. Valka cried for Peter Dingle and her insides that had betrayed her. My sister cried because life is hard and because she no longer had her beautiful hair and because she had something growing inside her that she already loved, she could just feel it. And we all cried for our insides and our outsides and the whole wide world.

When we were all cried out I took Jenny in my arms. I whispered that I understood everything she felt, or did not feel. That I was the same as her, that she was the same as me. She pulled back and looked at me. I promised to help her. But we had to get out of there.

Eventually it was night, pitch dark everywhere, and it started to snow again.

"If we are going to get anywhere tonight, we better get going soon," I said.

Valka stayed upstairs with Jenny to help her pack and I went downstairs to talk to my mother.

"Don't even start on me," she said, as soon as I walked through the doorway.

I walked to the refrigerator and popped open a can of beer. I sat down across from her at the kitchen table. I took the cigarette that was burning in my mother's trembling hand and I smoked it.

"How could you leave me?" she said.

"Oh, this is my fault?"

She looked down sullenly. She could not lie.

"We are taking Jenny away from you," I said. "You are done being her mother."

"You can't have her," she said. "She's mine." Her voice was caught up in her throat and all of the words were only coming out halfway. She was missing the beginning of some words, the ends of the others, and it sounded like one long noise.

"Mom, you cut her hair, you hurt her arm, you cannot keep her. You do not know how to be right."

"I know more than you," she said. "More than you ever will."

"I know enough," I said. "I know when it is time to leave. And it is time to leave."

"You'll never get rid of me," she said. I knew she was right. She was my mother. But I could fix it so that I was in control. All I had to do was leave. But I could not leave without asking one last question.

"Why can't I feel?" I said.

She shot her head up.

"You know. Down there. I have never been able to feel anything at all."

There was a weary smile on her face. She had gotten into our heads and ruined our insides. She had chosen to do it. It was her will.

. . .

HOW DID THAT STORY GO AGAIN? The one she always told me late at night, leaning over me. That smell on her breath. That look in her eyes.

Later on, he pushed her down on his bed and he lay flat against her and jerked himself off to the side. He picked up her arms and wrapped them around him.

Can't you just pretend you like it?

They slept for a few hours, and then, before the sun rose, he walked her back to the train. They did not look at each other, and there was no goodbye. She slid under the turnstile. She looked at the subway map. One transfer, and she would be at the airport. With her bruised face, with her swollen lip, she was sure they would let her fly home. Never to return.

She stood on the platform and waited for the train to arrive. A few businessmen joined her. A side glance at the young woman with the long blond hair and the messed-up face. The train pulled into the station. She sat down. She straightened her dress. She pulled her legs together. Her thighs stuck together. She pulled up her dress a bit and looked down. She was bleeding.

MY MOTHER PULLED THE BEER can to her mouth stiffly, first hitting the top lip as if it were lost, then sliding down to the bottom one. She drank and drank and it spilled a little down the corner of her mouth and down her neck. I watched the line of beer drain into her housecoat. Her eyes drifted, and then whatever light was in them before was gone. She put the can down. It was empty. She crushed it with her fist and the table shook.

She started to stand. I said, "Sit down."

"I want another beer," she said.

"No," I said.

"You get me another one," she said.

"Talk," I said.

She slumped down in her seat and flopped her hands on the table. She stared down sullenly, then jerked her head up at me and held her gaze on me for a while. Finally, she said, "You can't feel because you're not supposed to feel." Her words came out a slushy mess, as if she were wading through them in her mouth. What a wasted mess my mother was.

"I'm not explaining it right," she said.

"Figure it out," I said. "I can wait."

"You can't feel because if you feel it will hurt," she said.

"Mom," I said.

"Can I please have a beer?" she begged.

"No," I said.

She bent her head down, then said, very quietly, "I didn't want it to hurt anybody anymore." She slouched forward on the table, her head still down, and then held it up with her hands. "You were my little girls."

"That's right," I said. And then I spoke very clearly so

that she would understand—and so she would remember it after I had left—that what she had done was wrong. "We were just little girls."

Valka came down the steps with Jenny. My mother stood and I stood and pushed her down and she barked a noise at me.

"We are done here," I said. And we unlocked the dead bolt on the front door, the three of us crazies, and walked out into the snow.

25.

I had to do one last thing before we headed out of town. I was cold and shaking. I made Valka drive. The snowflakes were gigantic and lovely and we could barely see but I knew how to get there by heart. We rode slowly, past the last working stoplight before the railroad tracks, and down the barren back roads between farms. I blasted the heat. Jenny fiddled with the radio and she sang along quietly in the backseat.

"Couldn't we do this tomorrow?" said Valka. "Like when we can see. Like when we're not going to hit a snowbank and be trapped forever."

"No. Now," I said. "You made me come home, and now I am going to finish it."

Valka tightened her hands around the steering wheel. "If I die I'm going to kill you."

And then the snow stopped and it was fine, I could see everything clearly ahead of me. The cornfields were empty, it was just snow everywhere. There was not another car on the road. I was too excited to be done. I had never been done with anything before. I wanted to feel good. I wanted to feel right. I wanted to feel.

We parked in front of the home I used to share with my husband. There was a light on upstairs, and downstairs it was dark except for the flickering light of the TV. Jenny stopped singing and Valka tapped her hand on the window. The dog from next door came out with his limp, barked once, and then ran back behind his house. It was too cold out for even the animals.

"You're sure you want to do this?" said Valka.

"I've never been surer of anything," I said. Which was not really the truth but I was caught up in being a hero. It was my big dramatic moment. The end of my story in Nebraska.

There was no more waiting in cars for me. I got out of the car and opened the trunk. I pulled out the suitcase full of money. The suitcase from my honeymoon. A present from my mother. A goodwill gesture to get me out in the world, but also to make sure I was thinking of her while I was gone. Everything was rewiring in my brain all at once.

I slung myself into the snow, one foot after the other, until I reached the path Thomas had cleared. I held the suitcase tight in my arms. This is what I needed to do to be free. I laid the suitcase gently in front of the front door.

I stared at it for a moment. I nodded to myself. I would never darken this door again.

I walked back to the car and got in and slammed the door shut and it sounded nice and firm and final to me.

"Do you feel better now?" said Valka.

"Yes," I said.

"Did that give you the closure you need?" said Valka.

"I think so," I said. I took a deep breath. "Yes. I feel free."

"Good," said Valka. "Now, can you please go get that money back? Because otherwise you are flat broke. And if you're going to move to Los Angeles, you're going to need some cash."

"But—" I said.

"I mean, really," said Valka.

"That's a lot of money," said Jenny.

"Right! And what about that unborn child back there?" said Valka. "Who's paying for the baby food?"

"But what about closure?" I said.

"Oh, screw closure," said Valka. "I've got a good therapist you can call. Get your closure that way. Take the money and run, kid."

"Maybe you're right," I said.

A light turned on downstairs. Valka pointed at the house.

"You better do it now or forever hold your peace," she said.

I bolted out of the car, leaped through the snow, and grabbed the suitcase. Another light turned on, and the outdoor light, too. The last thing I wanted was to see that husband of mine. Like ever again. I ran back to the car, and when I slammed the door that time, it sounded even better.

"Okay, I get it now," I said.

"Must I teach you everything?" said Valka.

"Just shut up and drive," I said.

And so she did.

Epilogue

We all watched that show. Not a person alive in the U.S. of A. missed the series every Tuesday night at 8 P.M. EST for the three months it was on. *Rio: Undone.* How she almost died from driving under the influence in the early morning. How she wounded four Mormon parishioners visiting from Utah with her white Suburban. How she got off scot-free from jail because of the testimony of two people: a preacher and the head of a major studio. And there was the doctor who claimed she would never survive in jail because of her wounds. Rio could not remember a thing before the accident. There was talk of a lawsuit against another doctor who had given her prescriptions for a variety of medications that she did not technically need, but that faded, just like Rio's looks.

Because then there was the "undone" part. This miracle of modern technology could never have plastic surgery or another injection again. It would kill her, the doctors said. So everything she had ever done to herself started to undo itself, and she decided to let cameras film it. One week there were wrinkles around her forehead, the next around her eyes. Her lips shrunk down to thin purple lines. Her chin dropped into a jowl. The episode where she begged to get her hair colored had everyone laughing along. "I wouldn't want to go gray either," said Valka, whose hair had just started growing back in, baby soft brown and fine.

Her body—once it healed from bruises inside and out—was still in good shape, and her therapists insisted she work out, though she had to take it real slow. The episode where she ran a 5k for breast cancer helped raise an extra 100 million dollars in donations. At the end of the series, she was a forty-eight-year-old woman. Still beautiful, there was no denying that, but she looked exactly like she was supposed to look before she had started messing around with what God gave her.

"She kind of looks like my aunt Irinie," said Valka. "But without the stoop."

We watched her on the Emmys. Oh, Rio got lots of parts after that, not just for Lifetime but for the pay cable stations, too. She was the gray-haired grandma now in the TV movies, never the mom again. I did not get how forty-eight years of age equaled an old lady, but I do not make the movies, I only watch them. But it was her role as Helen Keller's teacher, Anne Sullivan, later in life, that won her

the Outstanding Supporting Actress award. Valka and
Jenny and I cheered her from our living room and threw
popcorn in the air. In her speech she thanked her agent, her
manager, Jesus, and blind people everywhere, who would
never be able to see her movie but would hopefully be able
to hear how much love for them she had in her heart.

That same weekend Thomas's penile implant stopped
working and he got an infection and almost died. It had
actually broken down a week before, but it took a few days
for the infection to kick in. He did not realize he was sick.
He passed out on the tractor and his fiancée found him in
the field. She ran around looking for him when he was late
for dinner, and gave him mouth-to-mouth and saved his
life. That was more than I could ever do for him.

His doctor pulled out the implant and told him it
was best if he steered clear of putting any other foreign
objects up there. He was back to the nub. When I heard
all of that, I called him and told him to send me the
divorce papers.

She can have him, I thought. Who am I to stand in the
way of love?

ME AND VALKA AND JENNY all live a fine life together in
Santa Monica. We go to the beach on the weekends. Valka
sits under a giant umbrella to protect her skin from the
sun. "I've had enough cancer for one lifetime," she said.
Jenny and I rush through the ocean like it is the most

amazing thing we have ever seen, and it is. It is wild and romantic and angry and free. Baby Laura squeals from the shore until we dip her feet in the water. I like that she is going to grow up near the ocean. Sometimes Paul Mc-Cartney comes in from Las Vegas and gives that baby the eye like he is trying to plant one right inside Valka. I wonder what she has told him and what secrets she has kept for herself. She does what she needs to do. I try to be the best friend I can.

Jenny is great in the shop. She deals with all the teenagers in town like a champ. They are her people. It is a relief for Valka, I think. We all keep an eye out that she does not get another bun in the teenage oven anytime soon. Next year she is taking floral design classes at the community college. Valka would be just fine expanding her floral empire with Jenny's help. I keep the books, stay in the back, away from any of the chitchat. I pray sometimes to keep my head together, because you can use prayer however you want. There are no rules one way or the other. Jenny and I go and talk to a therapist. We both agree it helps us just as much as the sunshine does.

LAST WEEK MY PARENTS came out for a visit. Jenny and I had huddled together and decided it was time for them to see their grandchild. Dad was struck dumb the minute he met little Laura. He sat down on the couch with her and got all quiet, and for a second I thought: that is it. He is really gone forever. But then he was on her with the toys and the cooing noises and he bounced her around and she laughed and adored him right back. Girl needs a grand-daddy like that. There was not a dry eye in the room. Even my mother, she rubbed at her eyes, caught a drip on her fingertip. Jenny steered clear of her, did not even lay a kiss on her cheek. It was fine. They do not need to be friends. They just need to give that baby love.

We played for a few hours, me and Dad and Mom and the baby. Jenny hovered, watching, and took the baby back just for feeding and changing. I think she let herself relax a little bit, especially when Dad was holding her. When the sun was setting we all went onto the back porch. Jenny and Valka stood off to the side, keeping an eye on me and Mom. We were drinking beer. Mom was smoking a ciga-rette. I took a drag. It was just like the good old days when I was still innocent and she was still an all right mother. Dad had cradled the baby up against him and was slow-dancing against the sunset. Jenny and Valka went inside to start dinner.

I asked for another drag, and Mom tapped out another cigarette from her pack. "Might as well just have your own," she said. She blew out a huge wave of smoke. "You know I'm no good at sharing."

Dad gave Laura a little dip.

"California dreaming," said my mother. She hummed to herself her own secret song. I wondered if she remem-bered that last conversation we had in my hometown, but if she did she wasn't showing it. That was fine by me. I never wanted to talk about it again, at least not with her. I had other things on my mind.

"All right, I guess I got a question," I said.

"Ask away," said my mother. "No secrets over here."

"What did you want?" I asked her. "With your life."

"You mean did I want to be Miss America or something?"

"We grew up thinking you hated us the whole time," I said. "Like you could have been something better, something fancy, if you had not had us to drag you down, to keep you in Nebraska."

She finished her cigarette and dropped it on the ground and stamped it out with the bottom of her shoe as if that cigarette had done her some wrong in life. She was thinking about what she was supposed to say. The words were not coming so easy. I did not know if that meant I was about to hear a lie or the truth.

"All I wanted was the two of you," she said. "All I wanted was to be married and to have children and to love my husband. That's how I was raised. I know I kicked up every so often—"

"Uh," I said.

"Okay, more than every so often," she said. "But to have happy kids who were healthy, that was my job, I knew it."

"I know you wanted something more," I said.

"What does it matter anymore, Catherine?" she said. "You got out. You and your sister both. Somebody did something right somewhere."

I looked right in her face to see if she was lying, but I do not know if that mattered either. It was enough for me that she wanted to believe it was the truth.

FOR NOW, I AM A SINGLE WOMAN, not alone in the world, but single anyway. I see how people look at me. They think they know exactly who I am because I am on my own. But I look back at them, too, with my single woman eyes. There is no one else telling me what to think but me. I am open, but careful. I pay attention. I am learning all the time. There is a lot to learn. I have a lot of work to do. Because I want to become the best version of me. The version I do not even know yet.

Someday I will be ready to look for love again. That is what I wanted forever, love, pure and simple. I could not find it with Thomas nor with any stranger I have met yet. And when I am ready to emerge from this cocoon of doctors' offices and ledgers and the strong scent of roses and orchids, I think I will rise like the sun. Brilliant and mighty, I will blind someone with my love.

But I am in no hurry.

This book would not have been possible without the generosity of Art Farm Nebraska and Ed Dadey. A million thanks to this wonderful residency program hiding out in the cornfields of Marquette, Nebraska.

Thanks also to the following co-conspirators who help me to be a nicer person and a better writer: Whitney Pastorek, Sarah Balcomb, Cinde Boutwell, Wendy McClure, Kerri Mahoney, Bernie Boscoe, Kate Christensen, Catherine Hopkinson, Sunil Thambidurai, Mara Jauntirans, Rosie Schaap, Emily Flake, Hana Schank, Maura Johnston, Pauls Toutonghi, Amanda Eyre Ward, David Goodwillie, Joni Rentz, Aimee Lee, Samantha Pitchel, TD Sidell, Ryan Walsh, Kevin Keck, Timothy Schaffert, Lauren Cerand, Janice Erlbaum, Summer Smith, Sarah Bowlin, Megan Lynch, Doug Stewart, and Jon Stuyvesant. You are all an inspiration to me.

With love, as always, to my family.

Jami Attenberg is the author of *The Kept Man* and *Instant Love*. She has written for the *New York Times*, *New York*, *Print*, *Salon*, *Nylon*, *Nerve*, and other publications. A Chicago native, she lives in Brooklyn, New York. Visit her website at www.jamiattenberg.com.